USSR

USSR

DIARY OF A
PERESTROIKA KID

VLADIMIR KOZLOV

Translated from the Russian by
Andrea Gregovich

FICTION
ADVOCATE

FICTION
ADVOCATE

A Fiction Advocate Book
FictionAdvcoate.com

Cover and interior design by Matt Tanner
Matt-Tanner.com
Composition by Susan Leonard
Rose Island Bookworks.com

978-0-9899615-1-6 (paperback)
978-0-9899615-2-3 (e-book)

1 3 5 7 9 8 6 4 2

FOREWORD

The remarkable novel you are about to read presents as clear and authentic a glimpse of bygone Soviet life at its most ordinary and mundane as you are likely to find anywhere. One might consider it a fictionalized documentary in the form of a literary text that reconstructs a slice of daily reality in the modern era's Atlantis: the old USSR. (I'm calling it the "old" USSR because right now it is back, to a degree, albeit in a new, mutated, and all-the-more fearsome, loathsome, and ultimately heart-breaking incarnation.) Other than Vladimir Kozlov, I can think of no contemporary Russian writer possessed of quite the same keen, unerring ear for the characteristic jagged pacing and sudden concatenations of "Soviet" parlance, or anyone gifted with a comparable sharpness of vision when it comes to the myriad minute details which used to define and regulate the comforting bleakness of regular Soviet people's existence.

The USSR occupied one-sixth of Earth's landmass and was sealed off all but completely from the rest of the world. It was a planet unto itself: a heavily militarized superpower populated by almost three hundred million people who were not, on first blush or in the end, all that different from the ordinary citizens of Europe, North America, or any other modern civilization across the globe.

(Now, it should be said that as one giant metaphysical whole, the Soviet people tended to possess a number of peculiar, idiosyncratic features and characteristics that set them apart from everyone else, such as their distinct propensity for viewing the world in strictly black-and-white terms, with no intervals of grey beclouding the ironclad certainty of their judgments; or their inherently fatalistic attitude toward the basic course of their own lives; or, say, their firm conviction that "compromise" is a dirty word and that those who happen to think differently from them on any issue of existential import are their sworn enemies and should be dealt with accordingly; or their near-total, child-like ignorance of the essential rules and principles of life in the infinitely mythologized West, the very idea of which they both loathed and loved—and that's just scratching the surface.) Despite their unique traits they were people like any others, and that makes sense, of course, because the areas of commonality shared by human beings, no matter the geographic, linguistic, or ideological circumstances of their birth and upbringing, are much larger and go deeper inside us than the isles of dissimilarity. People are mostly the same and generally unalterable in their essence everywhere in the world, and at all times.

By dint of his young age, Vladimir Kozlov spent only his childhood and adolescence in the old USSR, and therefore his take on Soviet life is necessarily that of someone whose comfortably small Soviet world, much to his confusion and the dismay of the adults populating the immediate confines of his small personal universe, has entered the zone of high turbulence. Before too long it will fall apart altogether, leaving in its wake the desolate, wide-open and wild vistas of an unaccustomed-to and generally unasked-for Darwinian freedom. Along with the rest of Planet USSR's populace, Kozlov's protagonists—which are in many ways his literary doppelgangers, for his fiction has a strong autobiographical bent to it—will soon find themselves thrust into this strange, frighteningly unfamiliar and post-apocalyptic terrain. Many of Kozlov's narratives are concerned with the quick, intuitive, and often misguided adjustments that ordinary Soviet people were forced to make on the spot in order to survive in their rapidly changing surroundings, even as they remained firmly rooted in their small, customary "Soviet" worlds, carrying those worlds along with them during the tumultuous transition like so many hermit crabs, if you will, hauling along their shells to hide in. Consequently, Vladimir Kozlov's view of reality in the last days of the USSR never arrives at a grand panoramic presentation: instead, it remains focused on the strategically chosen minutiae, the myriad details comprising those larger pictures and monumental vistas. He is a literary pointillist in the clearest and most artistic sense of the term, for his eye is almost unnaturally sharp, and his ear retains every single idiom of that dusky time in the past.

This bears taking note: perhaps the main distinguishing characteristic of ordinary Soviet citizens was their essential disbelief in their ability to manage the course of their own lives, to be the proverbial masters of their own fate. Their rulers were a given—much like the weather, say, which one is powerless to manage and can only adjust to (when it is cold outside, dress warmer, and when it rains, fetch an umbrella). All of us—Vladimir Kozlov, yours truly, and tens of millions of others like us – belonged to that unquestioning lot of Soviet people. We were the ones who never spent much time or mental effort contemplating the possible reasons our lives were the way they were: so poor, and so deeply isolated from the rest of the world. We were all denizens of that peculiar combination of kindergarten and boot camp that was the USSR. Vladimir Kozlov —the natural master of beautifully subtle understatement, tellingly unassuming knowledge, and thorough atmospheric observation—is the perfect chronicler of that odd Soviet world, that strange Soviet life.

This is a beautiful novel, skillfully and, indeed, beautifully translated by Andrea Gregovich.

Welcome to Vladimir Kozlov's time machine.

–Mikhail Iossel

INTRODUCTION

W hen Vladimir Kozlov wrote this novel, he aimed to capture the essence of childhood in the late days of the Soviet
Union in a way that would resonate with readers across the former
USSR. Kozlov is often asked if he is nostalgic for the Soviet Union,
but in fact the nostalgia of this book pines not for the politics
or ideology of its era but for the author's own childhood, which
happens to be set in a pivotal moment of history. While politics
certainly cast their shadow on the daily lives of Kozlov's characters,
politicians and their policies are only the backdrop for a more universal story of a boyhood just before the collapse.

USSR is set in Mogilev, a city in what was then the Belorussian
Soviet Socialist Republic. Mogilev is both a template-based Soviet
community and a locale with its own unique qualities—an indus-
trial city in a smaller republic with a landscape of forests and
farmland bordering Poland, the Baltics, Ukraine, and Russia. The
Belorussian Republic was one of the USSR's more affluent regions,
though its proximity to Chernobyl had a devastating impact on a
significant portion of its land. In the years since the collapse of
the Soviet Union, Belarus has become a strange hybrid of social-
ism and capitalism. Since 1994, the country's president has been
"Europe's last dictator" Alexander Lukashenko, who is known for

his sometimes violent suppression of his opposition and their political speech. The country still enjoys wealth thanks to Lukashenko's clever maneuvering for a portion of oil and gas transit from Russia to Western Europe. This wealth has allowed Lukashenko to build a regime similar to what Gorbachev had hoped to build for the USSR with free education and healthcare, collective farms and tractor factories, but no real communist ideology.

During Perestroika, though, Mogilev felt like just another Soviet city in an uneventful part of the USSR. Signs of a crumbling society were everywhere but childhood forged on, largely structured around the daily schedule of school and activities such as clubs, sports, Pioneers and Komsomol (the mandatory youth and teenage communist organizations). The required school uniforms were identical throughout the Soviet Union, leaving no room for personal expression: dark blue suits for boys and brown dresses for girls, with somewhat less drab dress uniforms for special occasions. The dry, dogmatic focus on schooling, structured activities, and ideology led to a healthy undercurrent of rebellion in cities across the USSR, even among good students like Igor, this novel's perestroika kid. The slow trickle of Western ideas, styles, and products into the Soviet Union intrigued the younger generations, and the breakthrough of rock and roll music was a powerful agent for ideological change. Only the most innocuous local and foreign musical acts were officially allowed to tour and record, and even they were heavily censored. Soviet rock music was entirely an underground phenomenon, copied and sold on the black market along with the Western music that managed to penetrate the Iron Curtain.

Product brands are prominent throughout this novel because of the heightened significance they carried in late Soviet culture.

Western products were scarce and Soviet products were limited in variety and of inferior quality, so people paid close attention to brand names, which were widely recognized throughout the culture even before advertising became a presence. As a sought after commodity, jeans became a prominent symbol of western influence during perestroika and of great interest to adolescents; the brands Igor mentions are mostly unfamiliar to Western readers because jeans available in Soviet stores were inexpensive imports from lesser known manufacturers. Cigarettes were also an important outlet for adolescent rebellion—in this novel we see the low-end filter-less brands *Belomor, Prima,* and *Astra,* which went for 20-25 kopecks a pack, and the most expensive status symbol brand *Kosmos,* a pack of which sold for around 60 kopecks.

Perhaps because they are of universal interest to boys, the few makes of cars and trucks on Soviet roads appear throughout this novel as well. *Zaporozhets* cars were so cheap and shoddy they were a common butt of jokes. *Lada* and somewhat less prestigious *Moskvich* both offered sedan and hatchback models. *Lada* also came out with the *Niva,* which is considered one of the few successful ventures of the Soviet automotive industry: the first SUV crossover in the Soviet Union and among the first of that type of car in the world. Out of range for average citizens, the *Volga* was a business-class car and was sometimes used as a taxi, and the *Chaika* was a kind of limousine used only by top government officials. Heavy duty trucks are notable in the text because their names are mostly acronyms that begin with a place name and end in "AZ", which stands for *Avtomobilni Zavod* ("Automobile Factory"), arriving at names such as *KamAZ* (from a factory on the Kama River in Tatarstan), *MAZ* (from a factory in Minsk), and *GAZ* (from a factory in Nizhny

Novgorod begun when the city was renamed for the writer Maksim Gorky). *ZIL* is an exception—it stands for *Zavod Imeni Likhacheva* ("Factory Called Likhachev"), named in honor of its legendary director.

Beyond what we can describe in this introduction, *USSR* is chock-full of Soviet-era details unfamiliar to most English-language readers. We've added endnotes to enhance references that lose important cultural baggage in translation. Other references we feel sufficiently explain themselves in the text, and some others aren't noteworthy enough to annotate further. This novel was written in 2009, the same year then-U.S. Secretary of State Hillary Clinton gave Russian Foreign Minister Sergei Lavrov the gift of a big red "reset" button, a symbolic gesture aimed at stabilizing the relationship between Russia and the U.S. How quickly things change! As *USSR* goes to print five years later in English translation, news headlines are threatening sanctions, possible military conflict, and a new Cold War between our two countries. What was originally a nostalgic look at Soviet childhood now offers a valuable cultural perspective in the current climate of geopolitics. If we consider what life was like for young people in the Soviet Union toward the end of the last Cold War, we might better understand the public opinion of the adults they are today.

–Andrea Gregovich & Vladimir Kozlov

USSR

DIARY OF A
PERESTROIKA KID

VLADIMIR KOZLOV

Translated from the Russian by
Andrea Gregovich

**FICTION
ADVOCATE**

I walked behind my parents beside the train cars, trying not to fall behind in the crowd of passengers. Papa was carrying a suitcase, Mama a knapsack, and I had the bag with food leftover from what we brought on the train. It was warm in the early morning. It smelled of some kind of southern flower or tree—something that wouldn't grow where we lived. The railroad came to an end just beyond the platform. There were square concrete planters with flowers in them at the beginning of every path. A neon sign was glowing above the train station: "City of Heroes—Odessa".[1] We had three hours before our commuter train's departure.

Chestnut trees with tall trunks were growing on both sides of the street. The street lamps weren't very bright—their light filtered by the leaves. Cats were crawling around in the dumpsters. Some of the balconies had blankets hanging on them to block the heat.

We came to a long staircase—it led up to the sea and the building marked "SEAPORT". A steamship was moored to the side of the seaport. The red sunrise emerged from behind a cloud. I unlatched my black leather camera case, took out my camera, set the distance to "infinite", and the aperture to "sun". I captured a piece of cloud with the sun and half of the mooring line in the frame. I pressed the shutter release.

Mama and I were waiting by a door marked "ADMIN-ISTRATION". There were letters stenciled above the door: "Distance to Minsk—1136 km." Yellow flowers were blooming in an old *MAZ* truck tire painted white. By the fence there was an old refrigerator truck the kitchen was using. Beside it there was a wooden shack with a "DINING ROOM" sign on it, and behind that were barracks of the same construction. Attached to the gate was a white sign with red letters that said "LIDA RESORT". Papa told me the resort wasn't named in honor of some girl but for the city called Lida in the Belorussian Republic, where we were from. A light fixture factory in that city originally built the resort so its workers could have a place to stay in Odessa. Then after a while they let anybody spend their holiday there.

The administration door opened and Papa came out.

"It appears we will be staying with a neighbor," he said.

"What do you mean, a neighbor?" asked Mama.

"There are no three-bed rooms, but one four-bed."

"So somebody else will be moving in with us?"

"He already moved in," Papa said.

A guy in shorts and a t-shirt with an Adidas crown logo on it was sitting on the bed in the corner. He got up, looked at us, and smiled.

"My apologies! This is quite a situation, isn't it? I'm rather embarrassed to be assigned to a room with a family in it."

"It's alright, not a big deal. We'll survive these twelve days somehow," said Mama. "It turns out they just have this policy here—all the rooms are for four people." She turned back to Papa.

"They didn't say anything about this at the factory?"

"Not a thing. And the voucher didn't say anything about it."

"Actually, they do have more than just the four-person rooms," said the guy. "There are some rooms for two. But you can only bribe for those. They aren't for regular stiffs like you and me."

"What do you do for a living? Are you a student?" asked Mama.

"I've completed my studies already. This past year I graduated from the philology department at Grodno University. Now I'm living in the town of Mosty. Maybe you've heard of it? It's in the Grodno oblast.[2] That's where I was assigned. I completed the practicum at my own school," he smiled. "That was a debacle. I gave a bunch of the honor medalists fours when they were supposed to get fives. I thought they were going to kick me out and I wouldn't pass the practicum. But it all worked itself out."

"Well, that's a coincidence," said Mama. "You and I are colleagues. I teach Russian in Mogilev."

"You don't say! That is quite a coincidence. You're a teacher too?" he turned to Papa.

"I'm an engineer," said Papa. "I work in the documentation department at an elevator factory."

"Please forgive me, I never introduced myself," the guy said. "I'm Sasha. But some call me Shurik and it doesn't bother me. I loved that character in *Operation Y*. That's a good movie. Really funny."[3]

★

At the spot where you were supposed to pose for pictures there was a fat lady in a black bathing suit sitting on a wooden dolphin with "1984" written on it in peeling paint. A photographer

3

was squatting in front of her, turning his lens.

The family from room fifteen was tanning next to us on the beach—parents and a kid with short hair and fresh scratches on his cheeks, from fighting, probably. He was about as tall as me. He was leafing through a magazine with pictures in it: steamboats, airplanes, cars.

"This is *Model Enthusiast*," the kid pushed the magazine at me. "Take a look, if you want."

There was a photograph of a fighter jet and its blueprint on the open page.

"You can make this by yourself?" I asked.

"Yes, but not at home, at a club. I'm in the aero model club. In Minsk where I'm from. And I collect model airplanes," he said. "My name is Ruslan. What's yours?"

"Igor," I answered.

"Where are you from?"

"Mogilev. I have airplanes too, but just a few. I mainly have model cars."

"What kind of airplanes?"

"A Treedent—"

"*Trident*," he interrupted.

"Supersonic Interceptor-Destroyer."

"I know that one—it's actually a MiG-21. They just didn't write it on the box. It's prohibited for them to print the names of war planes," he said.

"Why would that be prohibited?"

"So if an enemy sees the model, they won't know it's a real plane. They'll think it's just a toy."

"What enemy?" I asked.

"A CIA agent, for example. Do you know what the CIA is?"

"I know what it is. Are there really a lot of them around?"

"Who?"

"CIA agents?"

"I doubt it," he said. "In Mogilev you might not even have one. But there really are some in Minsk. Minsk being the capital of the republic and all."

Mama was rubbing kefir on my back. I got sunburned today. The door of our room was cracked. Papa was smoking and talking with a guy from a neighboring room.

"I try me them sardines," said the guy. "In that shop, over yonder." He pointed. "And boy, not very tasty, those. I reckon, with the sea being nearby, they shoulda been good."

Papa nodded, flicked away his butt and came back in the room.

"Is he from out in the country?" I asked. "Why does he talk like such a hick?"

"Quiet, you!" said Mama. "He might hear you."

Papa shut the door. "Yes, he's from the countryside. He's the director of a collective farm, not far from us in fact, in the Mogilev oblast, the Shklov district."

"So he and his wife get to stay in a two-bed room," Mama said.

"At first I didn't understand what he was saying, which sardines he was talking about," said Papa. "We went in that store three times and there weren't any sardines. And then I figured out he was talking about some canned anchovies. Those were his sardines."

All three of us laughed.

5

"What about you, Papa? Could you maybe be the director of a collective farm?" I asked.

"What do you mean, 'maybe be'? What for?" he said.

"In theory, I mean. They'd give us a two-bed room here with an extra bed for me."

"That's not my line of work," Papa shook his head. "I don't have the collective farm attitude. I'm an engineer."

"Well, what about factory director?"

"I could, theoretically," said Papa.

"Really?" asked Mama. "When might that happen? How much longer do we have to wait?"

"Ask me an easier question," he said.

Ruslan and I were walking along beside the sea next to the hotel's wooden barracks. The bridge and some port cranes were up ahead of us.

Something started whistling, making a noise, and then three fighter jets shot over the beach.

"The border's not far from here," said Ruslan. "That's why they're flying."

"The border with who?" I asked.

"Turkey. Didn't you take geography in school?"

"I took it."

"Do you know which of the countries bordering the USSR are really dangerous?"

"I don't know. China?"

"Why China?"

"Well, I remember when China invaded Vietnam. Brezhnev said we would wipe them off the face of the earth if they didn't leave," I said.

"I didn't know about that," he said. "But a really dangerous neighbor is Norway because they joined NATO. You know what NATO is?"

"I know NATO," I said. "Who told you they're really dangerous?"

"The geography teacher at school."

"So you really like geography?" I asked him.

"Yeah, sort of," he said.

"I have an uncle who's a geography teacher. Are you good in school?"

"Yes, in the primary subjects. I got fives this year except in Russian and Belorussian I got fours. What about you?"

"I got 'Model Student'," I said. "Half fours, half fives."

"Have you ever been to Minsk?" he asked.

"Once. Papa rode with someone from his factory who was rooting for Dynamo Minsk at a hockey game and he took me with him."

"I'm not a hockey fan. Soccer either."

"I'm not a fan either," I said. "But we didn't go to the hockey game. The other guy from the factory went but we went to the war history museum and then we went shopping. We bought sausages and candy."

"Wasn't there any sausage where you live?" he asked.

"Sometimes, but not very often."

"Was there no candy either?"

"Oh no, there was candy—chocolate bars, some with caramel and toffee. In Minsk we bought a really big *Stolichni* chocolate bar.

You know the one I mean? Also chocolate truffles. We don't have those at home. A long time ago, way back when I was still in kindergarten, Papa came home from Minsk with little liquor bottles made of chocolate. The box was the kind that usually had candy in it but this one had the little bottles wrapped in foil. Did you ever have those?" I asked.

"Yeah," he said.

"Do they have them now in the stores?"

"Sometimes, but I haven't seen them for a long time."

We came to the end of the hotels. Then we went up to the bridge that crossed between the sea and the estuary. A soldier with a machine gun was standing in a booth over the bridge. Next to it was a trio of Ganz cranes in the cargo port. The cranes weren't doing anything.

"How long before the bridge goes up?" Ruslan asked the soldier.

"About five minutes. Got a cigarette?"

Ruslan shook his head.

"What about you?" the soldier looked at me.

"No," I said. A tugboat floated toward the bridge on the estuary. It was pulling a huge barge full of sand.

"What about Pepsi Cola? Do they sell that where you live?" Ruslan asked me.

"Nah. Very rarely," I said. "Where do you live in Minsk? Which neighborhood?"

"You know the neighborhoods in Minsk?"

"No, it's just interesting to me."

"I live in Serebryanka," he said.

"I live in Worker's Village," I said.

"It's actually called that?"

"It's official name is the Kuibishev Settlement, but everybody calls it Worker's Village or just 'Worker's.'"

The middle part of the bridge lifted straight up from its pillars. I'd never seen such bridge. In a movie once, I saw a raised bridge that was in Leningrad but that one was quite different—the bridge broke in half and the halves lifted up.

Papa and Shurik were sitting on their beds, a board with small magnetic chess pieces set up between them. I sat on a chair and watched their game. Papa was winning—he still had his queen and Sasha had only his rook left.

Papa took a bottle of wine from the nightstand and poured half a glass for himself, half for Sasha. They clinked glasses, took a drink, then set their glasses on the nightstand.

"Check," said Papa.

The door opened, Mama came in.

"Well, how was Kishinev?" asked Papa.

"It was a whirlwind tour. An excursion around city for two hours, then two hours at the store and then back. Are you drunk?" she asked him.

"We're not drunk, we're engaged in cultural entertainment. We're playing chess."

"Don't think I don't see how you're playing."

"Did you buy cognac?" he asked her. Mama pulled a bottle of White Stork cognac from her bag then hid it back again. "But you won't be drinking it today, you're doing just fine with your wine. You shouldn't mix the two, you'll get too drunk."

"How come you get to decide for us? Maybe we would like to try some Moldovan cognac. What do you say, Shurik?" Papa said.

Shurik looked up from the board.

"Well, generally speaking—as a rule, I don't drink that stuff. Well, you might say I can have just a tad. If I'm in good company, for example. But on the other hand, there are good reasons why I wouldn't touch it. Maybe I should just go ahead and have some?" he smiled.

"You can mix cognac and wine," said Papa. "I read it once in a magazine. They're both from the vineyard so they're the same kind of spirit. It's wine and vodka you can't mix."

"You just made that up," said Mama.

"Cognac is a special beverage," Papa continued. "You can't touch vodka at all when you're drinking it. The same goes for wine. In '75 I went for a holiday in Gagra—not far from here in Abkhazia. Staying with me at the resort was a man named Lenya from Minsk, head of the supply department at the tractor factory. He was quite well versed in cognacs. On the first day he and I went to a restaurant to commemorate our arrival, you might say, and we ordered a bottle of cognac. The waiter brought a bottle, poured some in a glass, and Lenya tried it and said: 'Listen, dear friend, we are guests here, your brothers from White Russia, and we really want to knock back some fine Georgian cognac. What can you bring us?' He took that bottle right back and brought out the good stuff instead."

"Oh, I can't forget," said Mama. "There's a little something for you, Igor." She reached in her bag for a cardboard box and gave it to me. I opened it, inside was a Moldavian Pyramid, like a Rubic's Cube only triangle-shaped.

"Thanks," I said. "I've wanted one of these for a long time."

"They're interesting, all these gadgets," said Shurik. "But so complicated. We used to have a Rubic's Cube in the dorm. I tried it once, twisted and twisted the thing for maybe fifteen minutes. I couldn't figure it out."

"But it's so easy, you don't have to figure it out," I said. "You just need a diagram. Mama got a *Science and Life* magazine from the library, and it had a diagram."

"Listen to you," said Shurik. "Talking about diagrams."

Our commuter train was heading back along beside the sea. It wasn't quite eight in the morning. There was a *Lada* parked next to two tents on an empty beach. A guy in swim trunks was building a bonfire. Two others were still swimming. The sea was calm, almost no waves, light by the shore and dark on the horizon. Far, far out on the horizon a steamship was sailing by.

A father and daughter were sitting opposite from us, sunburned, and with their things. It looked as though they'd already been on their holiday. The daughter was probably around the same age as me. She had on genuine jeans, well worn, and a dark blue t-shirt.[4] I was looking at her. She turned away and got up to look out the window.

"For some reason I'm tired from this holiday," said Mama. "I wish we went home sooner."

"I, on the contrary, could have stayed a week or two more," Papa smiled. "The sun, the sea, what else do you need? And you, Ljuba, have nothing to complain about. You didn't have to make

11

dinner, you didn't have to clean up."

"That's the only thing I didn't have to do—make dinner. But I had to stay in the same room with a strange man. Is that a good thing? And I couldn't have a normal bath—the shower had no hot water. What about that, is that a good thing? No, I didn't need to go to the sea, it would have been better to go somewhere with modern accommodations that wasn't so far away," she said. "And what about you, Igor? Would you stay longer at the sea if you could?"

"Of course I'd stay," I said.

In the bathroom I laid out a sheet of plywood covered with oil-cloth across the bathtub. On it I arranged my enlarger and red lamp with the trays of developer, water, and fixative. There was one more tray for the final wash standing in the sink.

I started taking pictures in the photography club at school. The shop teacher Vladilen was the club's director. I went to that club for the whole year, all of fifth grade. They issued each of us a *Smena* camera and one roll of *Svema* 65-speed film every month. At the end of the month we developed our film and made prints in the bathroom on the third floor, which Vladilen had turned into a darkroom. At the end of fifth grade my parents bought me my own *Smena* camera and an enlarger. I put a sheet of photo paper under the enlarger inside its border, slid the red lens to the side, counted to three, pushed the lens back, and dropped the paper into the developer. An image began to develop: Mama and me with the Odessa Opera Theater in the background.

I pulled the glossy photographs from the ferrotype plate and gave them to Natasha. She examined them then put them down on the table.

"I'm jealous," she said. "You got to go to the sea. Not to that moronic work camp. All month long I had to dig in the dirt and weed beets. What a crock."

"Maybe next year we can all go together," I said.

"Next year I have to take the university entrance exams."

"Well, then, when you're in university. In August."

"If I get in," Natasha said.

"You will. The automotive institute has a shortage of students, for one thing," I said.

"How do you know?"

"Uncle Zhora told me."

"And how does he know? Does he work there now or something?" she said.

"Sort of—his friend works there."

"As far as I know there aren't any shortages at all. Everybody wants a degree. Even though you don't get anything for it. A teacher or engineer makes less than any laborer."

"Why is that?" I asked her.

"I don't know. Maybe because we live in a dictatorship of the proletariat," she said.

Natasha, Papa, and I were leaving the *Kulttovary* electronics store by the Motherland movie theater. I was carrying a box with a *Belarus-301* tape deck in it. There was a placard for an Indian movie called "Disco Dancer" up at the Motherland. It had been running for three weeks already.

Papa asked, "Well, are you happy with your tape deck?"

Natasha nodded.

"Make sure you finish tenth grade with all fives," he said to her.

"I'm really trying. It's not all up to me," she said.

"Who else would it be up to?"

"The teachers."

"You don't have to be a smooth talker, you know. If you know the material, there isn't a single teacher who can fault you," Papa said.

"Ah, but that's just not true," I said. "Some of them love asking trick questions, things you can't possibly answer."

"Then you need to figure out how to be the one they don't ask. Well then, you head home—I still need to run one more errand."

"Okay," said Natasha.

Papa turned on Pioneer Street. Natasha and I walked past the funeral parlor and the *Dom Buita* shopping center then came to First of May Street.

"What stuff are you going to make copies of?" I asked.

"First thing will be *Adriano Celentano,* and also that group *The Rich and the Poor.* Lenka has the records."

"Where are you going to get cassettes?"

"I'll buy them," she said.

"Cassettes are in shortage," I said.

"It's not that bad. Remember last winter they were even on display in the glass cases? The *TDK* ones were eight rubles."

"That was last winter."

"So what? There might still be some somewhere," she said. "If all else fails, I'll ask Papa to get some next time he goes on a business trip."

★

I opened the wooden gate of my babushka's courtyard and pushed my bicycle through. My folks bought it for me three years ago—a green adult model from the Minsk factory. It still looked pretty new. I replaced the front reflector with a plastic sniper soldier. Besides that I had four gold reflectors on the spokes of each wheel and another reflector on the rear fender. The fender I cut by myself from a piece of rubber I found by the trucking company. Sashka, Babushka's neighbor's nephew, was outside cleaning his crummy old fold-up bike by the water pump on the street. He looked at my bike.

"Why the hell are you showing off?" he said. "You won't be so special when you get all your reflectors ripped off."

Sashka was a year younger than me. He was in fifth grade at School #28. In first or second grade I had a little *Eaglet* bike and Sashka had his fold-up bike and we raced to see who was faster. The *Eaglet*'s wheels were bigger and I always outraced him, but Sashka would cheat; he'd go three meters farther than our agreed upon finish line and then holler that he'd won. One time I pounded him for it. Then Sashka snitched on me to his babushka, and she ran to my babushka and berated her for a long time. My babushka yelled at me, and I stopped racing with Sashka and pretty much stopped talking to him. At the beginning of this summer some of his friends came over—guys from sixth or seventh grade at School #28. They stopped by the water pump and watched me while I was putting air in my tires. One of them flung a stick at my back tire when I rode past them. He missed.

15

The street ended. The road on the right went to the engine repair factory and the railroad crossing. I turned left, picked up speed and rode up on the embankment. Across from the road there was a little path. Two ladies were tanning on a blanket on one side of the path. There were children running around them.

I rode down the embankment, coasting without pedaling for a long time, then turned left into the birch forest. A long time ago when I was still in kindergarten Papa and I came here on his old bike—me sitting on the cargo rack. When we got to the houses behind the Buinichi train station, Papa told me to keep an eye on the bike while he went off by himself somewhere. He was gone maybe forty minutes or an hour, and then he came back and we went into the village of Golinets to drink water out of a well. The water was cold and tasted good.

I rode out onto the road that goes to the oil storage terminal. The yellow grasses in the field were stirring in the wind. A cargo train approached the crossing: dozens of identical brown boxcars, then yellow and black tankers.

The doorbell rang.

"Can you get it?" Natasha asked me.

She was sitting at the table leafing through her books for tenth grade, which she had picked up at the school that day. I got up from the couch and walked across the room. The bell rang again. I stumbled over somebody's shoes in the entryway, caught myself on the wall, and then looked through the peephole. Uncle Zhora was standing on the landing.

"Who's there?" I asked anyway.

"Me," he said.

Uncle Zhora sat on the couch, opened his briefcase and reached for two *Spartak* brand chocolate bars. "Take these, kids they're yours," he said. "Chocolate is beneficial for mental work. That's a proven scientific fact."

"Thank you," said Natasha.

"Thanks," I said. "It's just the kind I like with the sugar-cream filling."

"You don't like the ones with chocolate filling?" asked Natasha. "Next time Mama buys some I'll take yours."

"I won't give them to you. I like them with chocolate too, just not as much." I tore the paper off the chocolate bar, unwrapped the foil and bit off a piece.

Uncle Zhora went over to the table and picked up a geography book with the number 10 on the cover. "In two days I'll start teaching out of this exact same textbook to kids just like you—a bunch of slackers."

"We're not slackers," I said.

"I know. Can't you take a joke?"

"I can take a joke."

"How's your tape deck? Does it still work?" asked Uncle Zhora.

"Well, yeah," I answered. "Are you suggesting it's going to break?"

"I don't trust domestic technology. Even less if it's made in our city. The only good tape decks are Japanese. The ones they make around here are pieces of crap. They're tape decks in name only."

"I'll bet you'll tell that to Mama and Papa," Natasha smiled. "It's a good thing they already bought this one."

"I don't have to tell them, they know it themselves. But they operate within their resources, which is in fact very wise of them. Just think, Natalya, in just two years you can buy yourself a decent machine if your heart desires. You'll join the youth work corps after your first year—"

"Oy, Uncle Zhora, let's not think ahead like this—I have to get in first," she said.

"You'll get in, don't worry. What have you been recording for yourself?"

"Just a few things so far. Toto Cutugno, Celentano, The Rich and the Poor."

"All Italians. What's that about?" Uncle Zhora asked.

"What's wrong with that?"

"There's so much good music—The Beatles, Deep Purple, Led Zeppelin—and all she listens to is the Italians," he said.

"Everybody's listening to them right now," said Natasha.

"Do you listen to them because everybody else does? Or do you actually like them?"

"I like them for the most part," she said.

I went over to the window, pushed aside the lace curtains and looked down at the street. A bulldozer with its scoop all covered in reflectors was driving toward the Green Meadow trolleybus terminal.

"How long before your mama gets home?" asked Uncle Zhora.

"She's at the district conference today," said Natasha. "She might be late because of it."

"Alright then, I guess I'll go. Tell her 'hi', and your papa—and

Happy Knowledge Day. Did you know that September first is now a holiday, Knowledge Day?"

"What does that mean?" asked Natasha. "We don't have to go to school?"

"No, Natalia, you still have to go to school. Why would the government let us take another day off?"

"But why call it a holiday then?" she asked.

"Well, we have Metallurgy Day, Tank Driver Day, Somebody Else Day," Uncle Zhora rolled his eyes.

"Well then, let there be Knowledge Day," Natasha said.

Guys and girls were walking toward the school coming from all different directions. Almost all the kids were carrying flowers. I turned away from the window. Natasha came out of the bathroom in her white lace school apron with matching lace collar and cuffs. She took a bouquet of gladiolas out of a three-liter jar—everybody in the tenth grade was bringing flowers.

"Did you forget your Komsomol pin?" I asked.[5]

"I did forget. I'm glad you remembered. I left it on my black apron."

"Will you tie my scarf?"

"Let me see it," she said. "Three years in Pioneers and you don't know how to tie a scarf."[6]

"I do know how. I just forgot over the summer," I said.

I grabbed my briefcase and left the apartment. Natasha had left ten minutes earlier. My folks bought me the briefcase in May, but

Mama said not to carry it until fall when sixth grade started. It was black, with simple locks made of shiny metal, no extra decorations. Inside it had a big pocket with a lock, three smaller pockets, and a little pocket for pens. I had stuck black electrical tape around the edges like all the other guys. If you didn't put the tape on the leather would wear down and the wood would show through.

Other guys stuck stickers on their briefcases with cars or babes on them, but I didn't put my stickers on the outside because I didn't want them to get torn. I stuck my own babe sticker on the inside. Babes were more expensive than cars and everything else. They were brought back by army guys who had been stationed in Germany. Guron from School #28 sold me mine, which he got from his cousin for a ruble fifty. Kolya was waiting for me between the apartment buildings. His briefcase was simpler than mine, but it did have the same lock. On both sides in all four corners he had it decorated with race car stickers.

There were linens hanging out to drying on Kolya's balcony—duvet covers, bed sheets, pillowcases, and somebody's pants and t-shirt. I whistled softly. Kolya came to the window and waved to me. I went in the entrance and ran up the two flights. Kolya was standing at the door. "Come in," he said. "Sergei's here."

I took off my shoes. We passed through the living room and into 'the children's room' in the far corner. Sergei, Kolya's brother, sat on the bed in a blue t-shirt that said "FOOTBALL". That summer he had started classes at Minsk Radiotechnical Institute. We shook hands.

"Are you here on a free day?" I asked.

Sergei nodded.

"How's Minsk?"

"Alright. Did you go there when the metro first opened?" he asked me.

"No."

"You haven't seen the metro at all?"

"Nope," I said.

"I really suggest you go see it. At first it made no sense to me. I looked around, really had to search for the punch machine, you know, to make the hole in the little coupon. Then I realized I didn't need to, I'd already paid with a token."

"How are your classes?" I asked.

"Don't ask! It's kind of like being in first grade again. We've only been there a week and there's so much homework already— physics and uppers."

"What's uppers?" asked Kolya.

"Upper level mathematics. Uppers, and history of the communist party. All you do is sit around studying," he said.

"How many people are there in your dorm room?" I asked.

"Three. The dorm is standard, new even, you might say. They built it not too long ago. And it's not far from the institute."

Kolya picked a pack of cards up from the table. "Should I deal for Thousand?" he asked.[7]

Sergei nodded.

I walked under the arch of the Great Wall of China—that's what we called a long building on First of May Street across from the *Dom Buita* department store—and went up the steps of School #16. A sign was hanging outside the door: "Citywide Office of Youth Engineers Model Car Club". I knocked.

"Enter," somebody yelled.

I opened the door. There was a track set up to run all the way around the room like in the game *Mototrek* only ten times bigger. Tables, a work bench, and a lathe were lined up by the wall. A bald guy with a mustache was sitting behind the tables in the corner. The hair on the side of his head was combed over his bald spot. He looked at me and said, "Were you born in a barn or something?"

"No."

"So then, what's the right thing to do here? You should probably say hello, don't you think?"

"Hello," I said.

"Look, I've got work to do," he said. "What you want?"

"Is this the model car club?"

"Yes."

"I want to join," I said.

"What for?"

"Just because. It's interesting. I collect model cars."

"Models are one thing, what we have here is something quite different," said the guy. "This is a sport. Like football or hockey, only the important thing isn't strength or speed—it's technical skill. Your head must sit firmly on your shoulders so your hands aren't always on your you-know-what. You understand?"

"I understand," I said.

"If you understand, then you need to decide whether this is

something you need in your life or not. I don't need the types who sign up and then come two times, and that's the end of it. Discipline is necessary here. We have a strict schedule three days a week: Monday, Wednesday, and Friday. There's always work to be done on these cars—soldering, sharpening the machine parts. What grade are you in?"

"Sixth."

"How are your grades?"

"Good."

"How good? How many threes have you gotten?"

"None."

"Are you serious?"

"I can bring in my grade book," I said.

"Alright, I believe you," he told me. "But that's not the most important thing here. An honor student you may be, but if your hands are like a girl's you're of no use to me. So should I put you down?"

"Yes."

He pulled a box out from under the table, took out an accounting ledger with a greasy cover, and opened it. "My name is Rogovets, Aleksander Grigorevich," he said. "I am the ranking champion in model car racing for the Belorussian Soviet Socialist Republic and trainer for the model car club. What's your name?"

"Igor."

"And your last name?"

"Razov."

"Well, look. If I put you down you have to work. I don't need any daydreamers here. This is a sport but with one big difference and that is mechanical skill. We compete a minimum of twice a year. First is track models in January." He nodded at the track. "This one's just a children's toy compared to what we compete on. Then in April there's regionals for cord models in Bobruisk. In May we have republic finals in Minsk. The team that wins the regionals goes there. If we win we go, if Bobruisk wins, Bobruisk goes."

★

The doorbell rang. I opened my eyes. It was still dark. The bell rang again, then again and again.

"Who could that be?" Mama said to Papa. "Go see what it is."

The bed creaked. Papa's white tank top flashed in the darkness. It rang once again.

"Who's there?" Papa asked from the entryway.

The lock clicked.

"Papa's drunk, he's hitting Mama." I recognized the voice of Olka Yakimovich from the fourth floor. She was a year behind me in school.

"Don't be scared, come in," Papa said to Olka.

The door creaked open. Mama got up and went into the entryway in her long pink nightgown.

"Don't cry, Olenka, everything will be okay. Go in the kitchen. Do you want some water?"

The light went on in the living room the door creaked.

"What's going on?" asked Natasha.

"Nothing. Go back to bed," answered Papa.

"Do you think maybe Olenka should stay with us for now?" Mama asked.

"No, I want to go home," Olka began to whimper.

"Let her go," said Papa. "It sounds like everything's settled down already."

Olka left. Her slippers slapped against the steps.

Mama and Papa came back into the bedroom. I pretended I was sleeping.

"What do you think happened up there?" Mama asked in a whisper.

"The usual. He came home late, drunk. She started lecturing him."

"She probably wasn't lecturing him, she just asked him—"

"What's the difference?"

"Not much, I guess. Let's go back to sleep."

"Hey dudes, let us ride your bikes!" a guy yelled at me and Kolya. He and two of his friends were coming from the vocational school. All three were in identical gray uniforms, the kind they wore at that school. We sped up. The guys didn't run after us.

There were two tractors on pedestals by the school's club building, a wheeled *Belarus* and a *DT* with tank treads. The vocational school had classes for tractor and combine drivers.

We rode past the "LET'S IMPLEMENT THE FOOD RATION PROGRAM" sign and got off our bikes.[8] Behind the sign's red slats and white letters was a WWII pillbox bunker. It was half overgrown with grass. From up on the hill you could see the whole city: downtown with its Great Wall of China, the apartment buildings on First of May, the Kuibishev chemical factory, the neighborhood on the other side of the Dnieper, with its rows of identical grey nine-story apartment buildings, the river port and its cranes, two barges of sand by the shore, and the wooden houses of Grebenevo, a village-like neighborhood on the edge of the city. Farther out on the horizon there was smoke from the pipes of the chemical complex.

Kolya squinted.

"Are you having trouble seeing with your glasses?" I asked.

"Yeah, they're weak already. I need to order new ones."

"Do you want to go with me to the Model Car Club?"

He shook his head. "Nah. You know that stuff doesn't really interest me."

"You'd need to learn how to solder anyway," I said.

"I know how to solder. I'd rather make a radio or something like that. Why would I want to build cars?"

"What if they're radio controlled?"

"Do they have those there too?"

"I don't know, they might."

"Alright, we'll check it out," he said.

"Is that our pillbox or a German one?" I asked him.

"It's German. Our troops advanced from there across the Dnieper. And there were lots of these pillboxes, one was near the engine repair factory but they demolished it when they built the apartment building by the big window grocery store."

"Is it from the Battle of Buinichi Field?"[9]

"No, this was earlier, in '41. When the Germans advanced through this area. Over there by the memorial and Simonov's stone."

"I know about Simonov, my Uncle Zhora told me," I said. "Simonov fought there and then he became a writer in Moscow.

My uncle said he even had his own airplane. And then he wanted to be cremated when he died and for them to spread his ashes on Buinichi field."

"So did they?"

"I don't know, probably. They put up the memorial for him and all."

"Alright maybe we can go home now?" Kolya looked at his watch. His folks had bought him an *Electronika-5* digital watch not long before, the kind that came in a black plastic case. "There's a show coming on soon. *Eternal Calling*, episode five." [10]

There were five minutes left of the *polit-info* session they made us sit through after school once a week. I was drawing a car in the margin of my *Pioneer's Pravda* newspaper. Lozovskaya was reading a speech from her notebook:

"For the money it costs to construct a single submarine, half a modern chemical complex could be built, and for one fighter jet, half of a city for one hundred thousand people."

"Excellent, Tanya" said the teacher. "Very well prepared, everyone should follow your example. Can you see what happens in the world? You must never forget about this, not for a single moment. The threat of nuclear war is one of the biggest threats humanity faces today."

I looked up from my newspaper and glanced out the window. Kids from the after-school program were running on the asphalt. Two of their teachers were standing by the flagpole. The shop teacher Vladilen was loading lumber into the trunk of his *Moskvich*.

Sitting in the nurse's office, his mouth open out to his ears, was Shestakov from A class, since all students were getting dental work at school this week. They said our class would get our dental work on Thursday.

Natasha and Mama were sitting at the big table in the living room. Natasha was doing her homework and Mama was grading notebooks. For Mama it was teacher's planning day. She didn't have to go to school.

"Is it true there might be a nuclear war?" I asked.

Mama raised her head and looked at me. "It could happen," she said.

"So what, we're all going to die?"

"Well, we shouldn't say such things. People are fighting for peace, you know, against the arms race."

"But all the same, we could die," said Natasha.

"Aren't you scared?" I asked.

"For some reason I don't think about it," she said.

"And you, Ma, are you scared?"

"I don't know. If everything and everybody dies it's not scary. Alright that's enough about that. Better go wash your hands for dinner. I just warmed up the cabbage soup."

I grabbed the green sauce pot from the stove, ladled myself half a bowl, and threw a few pieces of potato back in the pot. Then I opened the refrigerator, took out a liter jar of sour cream, took off the lid, put one spoonful of sour cream in the cabbage soup, and then another. The spoon left a yellow imprint in the sour cream.

Mama was talking to Natasha in the living room. "There

should always be a certain degree of flexibility. It's school, not the army. Yes, I was the teacher on duty, but I can't keep my eyes on every single one of them. It's always possible that one is going to run off, it's first grade after all. They're fresh out of kindergarten. They can't walk around in lockstep all the time. They're still not used to it, they don't understand. What good is it to reprimand me over this?"

"Ma, you shouldn't take it all so seriously," said Natasha. "Don't take it personally. You get frustrated over every little thing."

"You think this is a little thing? The director lectured me in front of the whole school and you really think it's a little thing?"

"But what else can you do? Resign? Transfer to a different school?"

"You think it won't be like this in a different school?"

"That's what I'm saying," she said.

I was sitting on the chaise lounge in the nurse's office waiting my turn for dental work. The dentist—a fat lady—was drilling Kutepov's teeth. He jerked around in the chair and whined. The dentist turned off the drill and bellowed at him. "Are you a moron? Why are you twitching? You want me to slice up your whole mouth?"

I sat in the chair and gripped the armrests. My heartbeat sped up. There were pieces of bloodstained cotton in the spittoon.

"Open wide. How am I supposed to see when you're like that?" barked the dentist.

I opened my mouth as wide as I could. She started poking around in my mouth with a metal pick.

"So... You have a cavity, I need to put in a filling."

"Are you finished? You aren't going to drill any more, are you?" I asked.

"As many as you need, that's how many I'll do. Don't ask any more, is that clear?"

The dentist pressed on the pedal with her foot and the drill began to spin again. I clamped down on the chair. She shoved the drill in my mouth so fast I barely managed to get my tongue out of the way. The pain came right away. I gripped the armrests hard.

"That's it, you're all finished. Don't eat for two hours. Next."

I got up from the chair and went out in the corridor. A tenth grader was brushing her hair by the mirror across from the cloakroom. I'd seen her a lot around Worker's. She was always with a guy named Red who had finished school the year before.

"Did you have to get dental work?" she asked.

"Yes."

"Did it hurt?"

I nodded.

"I refuse to go in for my dental work, I hate it. I hate dentists. And gynecologists," she said.

Gym was our last class. We took turns jumping across the pommel horse and landing on old tarpaulin mats. On the long wooden benches sat Korsunova, Tarasevich, and Lozovskaya who were all excused. Timur Nikolaevich stood opposite the pommel horse in a black running suit.

We took our last turn jumping.

"Everybody, get the horse and the mats out of the way. Basketball time. First girls, then boys."

"Why are they first?" yelled Kravtsov.

Timur didn't answer. He went in his office and brought out a basketball.

"Line up! Count off one-two!" he yelled at the girls.

The guys dispersed to the benches.

The game was over. We went in the locker room, all damp with sweat. The team I was on won twenty-one to sixteen.

Kuzmenok pulled off his blue t-shirt and sat on the bench. Kirillov was changing clothes across from him. He already had his shirt buttoned. Kuzmenok got up and grabbed Kirillov by the collar right at his throat.

"How come you elbowed me?"

"When?"

"Under the hoop when I passed to Tolik."

"I didn't hit you."

"Are you messing with me? Come on, let's settle this."

Kirillov looked silently at Kuzmenok. Kirillov was bigger and taller, but scared. Almost all the guys were scared of Kuzmenok.

"Well then, let's finish what you started, or are you pissing yourself?"

Kuzmenok punched Kirillov right in the gut, in the nose, then kicked him twice. Kirillov cowered crying on the bench. Kuzmenok took his shirt from the hook. The top of his collar was ringed with dirt.

I was getting ready to go to my car club. I took off my stay-at-home sweatpants and put on my *Miltons* jeans, which used to be Natasha's. When the Italian *Rifle* jeans first went on sale at *GUM* this summer for one hundred rubles she gave me her *Miltons*.[11] Then Mama and I went to see a seamstress she knew in the new building across from the big window store.

Her apartment had one main room with a sewing machine in it and pieces of fabric lying all over the place. Mama and the seamstress turned away as I took off my pants and put on the *Miltons*. The seamstress took a piece of chalk and made a few marks. A little kid—a year old or younger—crawled out of the kitchen. He took a piece of fabric from the floor, shoved it in his mouth, and started sucking.

The tailored jeans turned out just the same, they were only missing the rear seam between the pockets.

A trolleybus came along almost immediately. It was an old one with two doors—middle and rear. It was almost empty. I sat by the window.

The trolleybus rolled along beside the school. Fifth grade class A—they went to class on second shift—were sweeping the street. The guys scooped up trash with shovels on the side of the road while the girls swept the sidewalk. Their head teacher, my math teacher, yelled something. The trolleybus went another hundred meters and braked, not making it all the way to its stop. There were stopped cars and people crowded in the way. The driver opened the doors. I got out and elbowed my way through the people. A little box truck with a delivery shell had crashed into a big *ZIL* truck. The front of the box truck was totaled—its headlights and windshield glass broken and fragments of glass were scattered in a pool of blood. The back door of the ambulance slammed. It drove away and turned on its siren.

In the spring a car hit a kid from the first grade by the Worker's bus stop. He was running home during recess to building #170, crossed Chelyuskintski Street on the red light, and fell under a *KamAZ* big rig.[12] This was on a Friday when we were sweeping the street after class. When we saw the ambulance and a crowd of people, we all threw down our shovels and brooms and ran to the bus stop. The teacher yelled for us to come back but nobody listened to her.

The kid had already been taken away in an ambulance by the time we got there even though he had died at the scene. Zavyavlova said his eyeball was lying there on the asphalt. We wanted to get through and look but they wouldn't let us. Our teacher came and herded us back to the school. Then she gave us all a zero in conduct for the week.

A guy in a blue jacket—I remember him, he used to go to School #17—bent down and picked up a mirror from the box truck off of the asphalt. It wasn't broken, just cracked.

"I can put it on my motorcycle," said the guy.

Guron was waiting for me by the beat up doors on the rear steps of the school. He wasn't in his school uniform, but instead was wearing Texas brand jeans with zippers on the back pockets, the kind you couldn't get in a store.

"Did you bring them?" he asked.

"Yes," I said.

"How many are there?"

"I don't remember. See for yourself."

I opened my briefcase and began to arrange my plastic soldiers, cowboys, and Indians on the steps. I'd been collecting them for two years; I traded them or bought them, the little ones for fifty kopecks and the big ones for a ruble or ruble fifty. Last year Tarasevich from our class told me they had the Indians for sale at *GUM*. I went but when I got there they were already sold out. They cost a ruble twenty for the whole set, twenty pieces.

Guron picked up every soldier and examined it. "A few are good," he said. "The one with two pistols, the one with a whip and the one with his hands up. The rest are shit. And nobody really needs Indians these days. They had them a while back in *GUM* and everybody who wanted them bought them. Basically, I can give you two cars for all of them."

He opened his bag and took out two small imported model cars in blue boxes with plastic display windows. "Matchbox" was printed on the boxes.

"Why are they so small?" I asked. "Model cars are supposed to be a larger scale, one to forty-three."

"What do you mean, so small? What size do you want?" Guron put his arms out. "Like this? If you want them, take them, if you don't want them, don't take them. And you can stick your Indians up your ass." I picked up the little models so I could examine them. One was a red Audi-Quattro, the second an old Citroen with antique-looking fenders. The side of the Audi was scratched.

"Look, it's scratched," I said.

"That's it, piss off. You're fucking with me. Give me back the cars and gather up your shit. I'll sell them to Kovalev from seventh A for ten rubles. You hear me? You know how much money he's got? His old man works at the chemical complex in the hazards department—makes five hundred rubles a month, maybe more. He gives Kovalev a ruble every day, sometimes three."

"Alright, I'll take them."

"Took you long enough. Am I gonna need to rough you up? One of these days I'll end up kicking your ass." Guron punched me lightly in the shoulder then started to gather up all the soldiers and put them in his bag.

"If I get some more like this would you buy them off me?" he asked.

"How much?"

"Ten rubles, I said."

"A good *Chaika* limo costs nine-forty," I told him. "It's a very expensive model."

"So what? These are better. They're imports."

"Like hell they're better," I said.

I woke up. It was dark. I could hear the noise of my parents' bed creaking. I softly lifted myself up on my elbows. My parents' bed and my bed were arranged with the short headboards back to back. Papa was lying on top of Mama and moving. They were both under the covers. I could tell what they were doing. I turned quietly toward the wall. Their bed stopped creaking. Papa said something to Mama in a whisper. I didn't catch what it was.

The wind began to howl outside. On the balcony, clothespins were clacking against each other on the lines.

★

"Today we will devote our hour in class to discussion of the film that you were all required to watch," said our head teacher. "What was the film, who can say?"

"*The Scarecrow!*" yelled Nevedintseva.

"And does anyone remember the name of the director? Who remembers?"

"Baranov! No, Buichkov!"

"Buikov, not Buichkov," corrected the teacher. "Rolan Buikov, the well-known producer of Soviet children's films. So raise your hands everybody who watched the film."

Everyone raised their hands except Kosachenko and Kuzmenok.

"And why didn't you two complete the assignment?" asked the teacher. Neither of them said anything.

Kolya and I went to see the film on Monday at the *Red Star* theater. It was about a girl who was different and got bullied by her classmates which was supposed to be really shocking. Compared to what I saw every day it wasn't the slightest bit shocking. I didn't like it very much. It was just a typical movie, and I didn't see the point of the whole class watching it and then discussing it for the whole hour.

"This is the sort of film people argue about, the kind that provokes discussion in our society," said the teacher. "We discussed it in our pedagogical collective as well, and the ideas expressed there were quite diverse. But I suggest that you focus your attention on one element, the key element as I understand it, and that is the interrelationship between the collective and individual man. The leading heroine—"

"Is it true she's Pugacheva's daughter?" asked Zavyavlova.[13]

"First of all, it's not good to interrupt when I'm speaking," the teacher said sharply. "But just so that we don't have to return to this subject—yes, Kristina Orbakayte is the daughter of our well-known singer Alla Pugacheva."

"Why does she have a last name like that? Is her papa not Russian?"

"I will repeat myself. We are not here today to talk about the actors who star in the film but about the moral and ethical problems that arise in it. But as I was starting to tell you before I was interrupted, one of the most significant problems is the interrelationship between man and the collective. The leading heroine does not fit into her new school's collective, and this is in large part her own fault because she doesn't understand the significance of the collective. She doesn't realize that the collective takes priority over its individual members. This is her true tragedy and misfortune."

"Is it true they make soap from dog fat?" asked Zavyavlova. "They said that in the movie."

The tractor was slowly pulling its potato combine across the field. We were walking behind it with a bucket, picking up potatoes. When the bucket filled up, we carried it to the other tractor, which had a trailer. An old guy in a cloth cap was standing on the trailer smoking a *Belomor*. He leaned over, took the bucket and emptied it into the trailer.

"Are you gonna go head to head with Kirillov?" Kuzmenok asked me.

"What for?"

"Because... He called you a bad name," Kuzmenok smiled. I could tell he was lying. "Come on, we'll go around on the other side right now so the teacher won't see."

"I'm not going."

"Are you pissing yourself or something?"

"I'm not pissing myself. I just don't want to."

"Now you'll say you have a headache or something, right?"

"I don't have any kind of ache."

"Then how come you're pissing yourself?"

"I told you, I'm not pissing myself," I said.

"So that means you will?" He smiled.

Kirillov hit me first—not hard, but right in the nose. The blood ran. I kicked him. I wanted to get him right in the balls, but I missed and hurt myself. I screamed. Kirillov stepped back. I got him again with my fist—under his eye and in the ear. Kirillov turned away, holding his face.

"Alright, that's enough," said Kuzmenok.

The bus drove along beside the gray fields. The big toe on my right foot hurt—the one I kicked Kirillov with. Kirillov sat by the window, Kuzmenok across from him. Kuzmenok snatched the hat off his head and shoved it out the window like he was going to throw it out. Kirillov jumped up on the seat and reached for it.

"What's going on back there?" yelled the teacher. "Quit fooling around right now."

The white letters of "MOGILEV" passed by out the window as we drove back into the city.[14]

I squatted in the entryway as I tried to pull off my rubber boot and sock. My toe was swollen. I tried to take a step but couldn't. I had to hop on one foot.

"What happened?" asked Natasha.

She was sitting at the living room table doing her homework. The eighth and tenth grades didn't go to the collective farm because they had to prep for exams.

"I was trying to kick potatoes out of the ground," I said.

"Don't feed me a line like that, okay? Who were you fighting with?"

"Kirillov."

"Why'd you pick a guy like that to get in a fight with? Aren't you ashamed of yourself? Everybody beats him up."

"He came at me first. Don't tell Mama and Papa."

"What are you gonna to tell them?"

"That I was playing soccer."

"With a potato?" she asked.

"Well, yeah," I said.

The front door slammed. Papa was leaving for work. I was awake already but I didn't want to get up. Mama and Natasha were in the kitchen eating breakfast.

"Why was he occupying himself with such nonsense?" said Mama. "Playing soccer with a potato! Where did he come up with such a thing? Now he gets to sit at home with a smashed toe excused from school."

"There's nothing terrible about being excused for a few days. What good comes from him being in that school?" said Natasha.

"You, his older sister, would say this? You should be setting a good example for him."

"And I show him one. In everything," Natasha laughed. "Well, almost everything."

I got up from my bed. I had a hard time pulling on my sweatpants with my toe splint, then I put on my green checkered shirt.

My breakfast of two sausage patties was in the frying pan on the stove. I set the frying pan on table, took my fork and stuck it in a patty. It was already cold. I opened the refrigerator, took out a new bottle of kefir, and poured myself a glass.

The morning news shows were on. *Time* was on channel four. I changed it to seven, *Morning Republic*. Out the window and across the street, the school windows were lit up: the third floor where my grade had classes had one chemistry classroom, two Russian, one Belarusian, one history, and two mathematics classrooms. The German teacher Semina was running from the bus stop. She wasn't our teacher but everybody knew she was psycho. Last year I left class to go to the toilet and heard her swearing at Odintsov from seventh A. He had looked into her classroom and asked to talk to Krilovich. Semina threw a piece of chalk at him. The chalk left a mark on Odintsov's jacket and fell to the floor, breaking into pieces.

Odintsov said, "You need your meds, loony."

"Go to the principal's office!" Semina bellowed.

"How dare you talk to a teacher like that?"

"And you shouldn't be throwing chalk at me. Let's both go to the principal, I'll tell him what you did. Or are you pissing yourself?"

The trolleybus rolled up to the traffic light. Out the window was the sculpture in the center of Ordjonikidze Square.[15] It was a guy and a girl. They were lifting up their hands, holding a *sputnik* together.

The light turned green. The trolleybus crossed Pioneer and stopped. I got out and turned on Lenin. I had only taken the splint off yesterday. My toe still hurt a little.

I went inside Toys. There was nothing interesting there. I'd bought lots of things there in the past: an amphibious jeep that floated in the bathtub and a *Piko* model railroad, which of course broke pretty quickly and the locomotive quit running on the track. I also bought some weapons there: a plastic machine gun with a red light in its barrel, a black *Mauser* pistol, and a little brown cap gun. In fourth grade and the beginning of fifth, I used to play war with some guys on the kindergarten playground behind the cafe that faced the street. There was a two-story structure on the kindergarten grounds that we called "the tower." It had stairs to the second story. To win a war game, one team had to "storm the tower."

The consignment shop had some new Japanese tape decks for a thousand rubles or more—Sharp, Toshiba, and Sony. They all had bright "25 W" or "Hi-Fi" stickers on them. People who traveled abroad brought them back to sell for a profit. There were always guys standing around them—young and old alike.

A little piece of paper hung on the door of the store. Written by hand on it was:

Automobiles for sale:
Zaporozhets-965—600 rubles
Zaporozhets-965A—650 rubles
Zaporozhets-968—2200 rubles

I couldn't imagine why anybody would want to buy an old *Zaporozhets*.

I opened the door and said "Hi."

The guys at the tables nodded to me. Rogovets looked at me.

"Where have you been, son?"

"I smashed my toe."

"Prove it!" yelled Potapov.

"I can bring in a note."

"You don't have to bring me a note. You're not in school here, everyone's here by choice. If you say you smashed it, then I believe you. Take your jacket off and get to work."

I took off my jacket and hung it on a hook beside the others. There was a photograph of last year's regionals pinned up above the hooks: the guys with their "Youth Champion" ribbons. Pika and Dodik were in the picture. They were sitting at a table that day soldering cars.

I went to a table and turned on a soldering iron.

The door opened. Shorty came in and looked around. He was two years older than me, but he was only in seventh grade because he spent two years in first grade.

"And where were you?" asked Rogovets. "You smashed your toe too?"

"No, I was making up a quiz. I got a two."

"In what?"

"German."

"German, that's good. I studied German at the vocational school. Two years. I even got a four in it for two whole years."

"Two two's for a grand total of four," mumbled Pika.

We all laughed.

"I don't remember anything. Just 'wie hast du' and 'kolchosbauer.' That means 'collective farmer.' But in school I took English. I remember how to say "bicycle".

Shorty stood by Rogovets' table holding his car, a *Metallex MTX* formula racer. He had only soldered half the body.

Rogovets brought out a box from under the table, took out a pack of *Astras* and pulled out a cigarette.

"Come're and light my cigarette."

Shorty took the cigarette and went over to the dish heater. I brushed acid on the side of the car, stuck the soldering iron in the can of liquid tin, and then put it on the car.

The room smelled of tobacco. Shorty was holding Rogovets' cigarette.

"Well, aren't you a *kolchosbauer.* I told you to light it, not burn up half the cigarette, you big dummy. A *kolchosbauer* on a bicycle, that's you."

★

Papa was snoring in the bedroom. He was drunk when he got home half an hour before, and he took off his clothes and laid on top of the bedspread in his red boxer shorts and a lime green tank top. His head was propped up high atop two pillows. When Mama made the bed, she always put the pillows in the corner, one on top of the other.

I sat at the table finishing my algebra. Mama went in the bedroom and touched Papa on the shoulder.

"Petya, get up. It's time to make up the bed."

Papa mumbled something, rolled over, and kept snoring. Mama touched his shoulder again, this time more forcefully. Papa turned his head and opened his eyes.

"Get up," said Mama. "I need to strip the sheets."

Papa stared at the door on the cabinet.

"How long am I going to have to wait for you? It's eleven o'clock already, time to make up the bed. Igor needs to go to bed soon."

"I'm not going to bed yet," I said.

"It's time. It's quarter to eleven already."

Papa sat up in bed.

"Do you not understand Russian?" asked Mama. "How long do I have to wait?"

"Not very long. In fact you don't have to wait for me at all. I'll get up right now and that'll be the last thing ever."

"Where are you going? Why would you say such a thing?"

"Go away, don't bother me." Papa put his leg down on the floor, looked at me, stood up, staggered, and grabbed for the headboard. Mama started to pull the covers off the bed. Papa picked his pants up off the chair. His belt buckle clinked and hit the headboard.

"Where do you think you're going?" said Mama. "Lie down. I made up the bed so you can lie down now."

"Enough is enough is enough. That's it. I'm leaving. To hell with all of you. Enough is enough is enough."

Papa zipped his fly and buckled his belt. He shoved his hand in the sleeve of his shirt.

"What in the world, Petya? What's going on? You can lie down now. The bed is made."

The door opened. Natasha looked in.

"What's going on in here?" she said.

"You get out of here, leave me alone." Papa tried to button his shirtsleeve. "To hell with you all. I'm leaving. I can't take it anymore! You did this to yourselves. I'm not going to worry about you anymore. Not a bit, you'll see. You'll all get it but it'll be too late. This is it for me. This is it."

Natasha hopped out of the way. Papa went out in the entryway, groped around for the light switch, and turned on the light.

"Do something," Natasha looked at Mama. "He's trying to leave."

"Petya, calm down," said Mama. "Lie down, the bed's made."

"Stop telling me that. And you can have my five hundred rubles. I don't need them anymore. I don't need anything anymore. Got it? That's it. I don't need anything anymore. Or do you still not get it? Enough is enough, I said. I'm leaving, motherfuckers! I'm gonna leave. Then you'll get it. But it'll be too late." Papa shoved his bare feet in his boots and started tying his laces.

"Papa, stop," said Natasha. "What's wrong with you?" She turned to Mama. "What is he talking about? What five hundred rubles?"

"How should I know?"

"Where was he today? Who did he get drunk with?"

"He doesn't report back to me, as you well know."

Papa stood up, which made him stagger. He took his jacket off the hook.

"Take your clothes off right now and lie down!" screamed Mama. "Why do you make such a scene with these episodes? Hey, I'm talking to you! Take your clothes off and lie down! I don't know what I'm going to do with you anymore!"

I was afraid Papa would hit Mama. He was sitting on the bench in the entryway, trying to pull off his boots.

"It's about time," said Mama. "It is unbelievable to me that you can make such a scene around the children. You don't care about them at all, do you? Don't you understand how you traumatize them with these episodes?"

Papa went in bedroom, drunkenly unbuttoning his shirt along the way. Mama went to him, helping him, then turned off light. Only the table lamp was on. I had one equation left to do.

It was snowing out the window. We were working in the metal shop filing spanner keys. We were doing them on procurement order for the trolleybus depot. Vladilen sat by himself in his office. He always gave the assignment and then went to his office. He just sat there reading his *Soviet Sports* newspaper.

The bell rang signaling the break between shop class sessions.

"Snowball fight!" screamed Kuzmenok.

The door to the outside was opposite the workshops. Kuzmenok opened it and jumped out into the snow. We all stayed just how we were—in slippers with our black shop aprons on over our jackets. Everybody started making snowballs and throwing them at each other. Vladilen looked out the window.

"Go farther out!" he yelled. "Don't you hit that window! God help you if you break it, you'll be fixing the glass yourself. Is that clear?"

We crowded around Vladilen's desk with our spanner keys—everybody except Kirillov, who was still standing at his workbench filing his spanner key.

"Kirillov!" yelled Vladilen. "Finish up right now! Everyone's waiting on you!"

Kirillov loosened the vice and took out his spanner key. Everybody snickered as they watched him. His key was crooked, like a technical drawing done without a ruler.

"Well, Kira, you guaranteed yourself a two," said Kuzmenok.

"How is that a two? It's a one," Strelchenko snatched the key from Kirilov. "You should probably just throw it in the garbage."

"Give him back his key," said Vladilen. "I'll be the one to decide what he gets. Give him back his key right now."

Kirillov grabbed his key back from Strelchenko. Vladilen beckoned with his finger, took the key and held it in his fat, scarred fingers.

"What in the world is this thing you made? This is a spanner key? If you can't be civilized about it next time I really will give you a one."

He took his pen and marked a three minus in his greasy journal. The minus line was almost a centimeter long.

★

I hung my bag with my slippers and jacket on a hook and took a little number tag—199. With a number like that I could play a good game of "Forty Lashes" with somebody—where the guy with the higher number gets to flick the other guy as many times as the difference between their tag numbers, but nobody played that stupid game anymore. We played it last year when there were new hooks with numbers in the cloakroom. Nobody tried to play it after first period because the good numbers were all taken by the class on duty.

The cleaning lady, Semenovna was pushing a mop across the tile floor. A bucket of water sat nearby. There was garbage floating in the bucket. A crowd was standing by the door to the stairs. The first bell hadn't rung yet so they couldn't get up to the second and third floors.

Kuzmenok was sitting on the corner bench.

"Hi," he said.

I nodded to him.

Kuzmenok opened his briefcase and took out his graph paper notebook. He always drew during classes.

"Razov, look at the soldier I drew. It's a decent soldier, yeah?" He couldn't really draw. All his soldiers looked like robots.

I said, "Yeah, it's decent."

"How is this one? Decent?"

"Uh huh."

"And which do you like better, this or this?"

"This one."

"Look over there, that's the guy who robbed the buffet," Kuzmenok pointed at Shchukin from tenth A. I'd heard about that, Natasha told me. A month ago on a Sunday, Shchukin and Gorshkov from his class broke in through the door of the buffet and took some money—twenty-five rubles and forty-six kopecks. But then the buffet lady Lilya Petrovna caught them on their way out since she happened to be stopping by the school. The whole thing was hushed up because Shchukin's papa was the head of the trade union at the tire retreading factory, and that factory was our school's biggest benefactor.

The bell rang. The on-duty guys from seventh B opened the door on the landing. The crowd lurched upward.

"Don't run on the steps!" called out Sofia Eduardovna, the small, gray haired-head teacher for seventh B.

The radio over the door crackled:

"Attention students, it's time to begin our morning exercises. First exercise: stand with your feet shoulder width apart and extend your arms to the side."

The history teacher sat behind her table leafing through a magazine and chewing on the handle of her glasses.

"Now we will do knee bends. Down on one, up on two. One two, one two..."

The history teacher looked up at us.

"Okay everyone, hands out of your pockets, we are going to do the exercises, and we're not just going to pretend we're doing them. You're the ones who need this, not me. So you don't just sit there during class like a bunch of sleepy flies."

★

I t was snowing. I stood at the crosswalk on Chelyuskintsi and waited for the cars to pass. The snow on the road was light brown from the mud on all the car wheels. A trolleybus went past—I could see a first grade teacher from my school sitting on it.

After I took off my boots and jacket I shook the snow off my coat, then hung it on a hook and went in the kitchen. Natasha was eating soup.

"Open the refrigerator, look what Papa brought for supper."

I opened the door and looked. There was a clear bag of tangerines on the shelf.

"Take two for yourself and leave two for me," said Natasha. "But eat your soup first, okay?"

"Okay."

Each tangerine had a little black diamond stuck on it that said "*Magos*". Last year Mama bought some oranges with the same sticker.

"The tangerines are from Morocco," said Natasha.

"I know. Why are they always imported in December?"

Drops of snow were sticking to the glass and the courtyard was already almost covered.

"They're probably harvesting them there right now."

"They must harvest them year round there. Morocco is almost on the equator."

"That I don't know. But who cares? We have plenty of apples in the summer, after all. And pears."

The dead air from the broadcast break ended with the transmission of the exact time message:

"In Chita it is nineteen o'clock, in Vladivostok it is twenty-one o'clock, in Magadan it is twenty-three o'clock, in Petropavlovsk-Kamchatsky it is midnight."

★

"Will you stand on a chair and stick the snowflake up there? You're taller," Zenkovich begged me. She was sitting at the teacher's table making snowflakes with notebook paper—rubbing them with a piece of soap and sticking them to the window. Zenkovich was wearing a black blouse and jeans—*Miltons* the same as mine, only new.

Other kids were washing the desks and the walls, and standing on a desk to hang tinsel decorations on the light fixture. Not everyone showed up for this cleanup project, which was always on the first day of vacation. Kutenov, Kuzmenok and a few others weren't there.

I pushed the chair up close to the window and stood on it. Zenkovich gave me a snowflake.

"Here or higher?" I asked.

"Maybe a little higher," she said.

I stuck the snowflake to the window, pressing it down with my fingers to smooth it out.

The teacher stood watching us silently by the door.

"What will happen to the kids who didn't show up today?"

asked Lozovskaya.

"This will lower their grade for conduct," answered the teacher.

"But progress reports for the quarter already came out..."

"So what? All of them will have lower conduct scores for the first week of third quarter."

"You say that every time but nobody's conduct ever goes down. Next time I'm not coming," Lozovkaya said.

Zenkovich gave me one more snowflake. I stuck it to the glass and looked out the window. A blue *Niva* drove down Gorky Street. An old guy was pulling a small sled behind him. Smoke was coming from the chimney of a country house. The contour of Zenkovich's breasts swelled under her blouse. She noticed me looking. I blushed.

The room smelled like pine needles. Papa shortened the trunk of the Christmas tree so it would fit in the stand. Natasha, Mama, and I unpacked the ornaments. They'd been in the pantry since last year in the old vacuum cleaner box. There were lots of ornaments—big multi-colored balls, transparent and sparkly, smaller balls with different patterns, little houses, fish, cars, and tinsel decorations.

Papa screwed the tree into the stand, moved it into the corner between the television and the table, and swept the droppings into the dustpan.

"Alright, you can start decorating," he said.

"Yes, it's time," said Mama. "And I still have some cooking to do."

"Well everyone, we need to turn it on," said Mama. "To see how it looks."

I hooked up the star to its battery—it was red like on the tower of the Kremlin. Mama bought it in *GUM* last year. Natasha plugged the lights into the lamp's outlet. The tree lit up.

"Splendid," said Mama. "Simply beautiful." She turned to Natasha. "What time do you leave?"

"Seven o'clock."

"Why so early?"

"We need to get everything ready."

"Well, you'd better make sure that everything goes well. You are almost adults, about to graduate and all."

"Don't worry. Of course everything will be fine," Natasha said.

Papa and I were sitting in front of the television. Papa was drinking beer from a big goblet, the kind he used for kvas in the summer.[16] A film about the hussars was playing, there were nineteenth century cavalry soldiers on the screen. Mama was tinkering around in the kitchen—I could smell roasting chicken. Natasha came out of the bedroom in her *Rifle* jeans and a dark red sweater with made up eyes and lips.

"Well, I'm leaving. Goodbye everyone. Happy New Year, best wishes!"

"When will we give her her presents?" I asked.

"She'll get her presents tomorrow!" Mama yelled from the kitchen. "Too early isn't any fun."

The four of us sat at the table: Mama, Papa, Babushka, and me. General Secretary Chernenko was on the screen reading his New

Year's wishes.[17]

"I'm getting the impression he was unconscious while they filmed this," said Papa.

"Don't ever say that anywhere else! Just in case." Babushka looked at Papa.

"Don't worry, don't worry, I only say it to my family."

"Happy New Year, good comrades!" declared Chernenko.

The clock face on Spasskaya Tower appeared to replace him on the screen. The chimes began to ring. Papa took the bottle of champagne, unwrapped it and took off the wire, and then slowly pulled out the plastic cork. The pop was just barely audible. He poured champagne in goblets—all of them full but just a little bit for me. On the television the fireworks began and the numbers "1985" appeared.

I opened my eyes. Papa was standing over me.

"Get up. Time for school. Vacation is over."

Papa went to the wall and flicked the switch. One of the two lamps came on. His and Mama's bed was already made. Water was running in the bathroom. In the kitchen the radio was on. I got out of bed, took my sweatpants and shirt from the chair, got dressed, and put my feet in my slippers, which had their heels crushed down. Natasha came out of the living room in her school dress and white apron, with a red armband. Their class was on duty at school so she had to go in half an hour early.

"Mom, I don't have time to make the bed, okay?" she said.

I went over to the window in the living room. The windows

were lit up at the school, in building #181, in the apartment buildings on Gorky Street, and its lanes. Beyond that, far, far away, there were tiny lights on the buildings on the other side of the Dnieper, just barely noticeable.

There was a plate of fried eggs waiting for me in the kitchen. Everyone else had already eaten. I didn't like it when my fried eggs were too runny and today they were like that. I took a piece of brown bread, opened the butter dish and spread some butter on my bread.

"We're leaving!" Mama yelled from the entry. "Lock the door good!"

"Alright," I said.

I took off my stay-at-home sweatpants, put on a different pair—also blue only newer—and tucked the foot strap into my sock. Some guys wore the foot straps over their socks but I didn't like them that way.

My school uniform, including the shirt, was hanging on a hanger in the entryway. Mama had ironed it the day before. I put on my shirt and my slacks over my sweatpants, fastened the buttons, went to the mirror in the bedroom, and tied my Pioneer scarf around my neck. The Pioneer pin on my jacket was all scratched— I'd been wearing it since I first became a Pioneer. In seventh grade they gave out new ones that said "Senior Pioneer".

Five minutes were left before Algebra started. Kuzmenok went up beside Kolya and did a finger leech on his arm.

"Knock it off," said Kolya.

"Are you talking to me?"

"Yes you. Knock it off."

"Are you gonna mess with me?"

Kuzmenok knocked Kolya in the shoulder. Kolya got up and shoved Kuzmenok back. Kuzmenok punched him in the jaw, then again in the nose, then in the glasses. Something cracked. His glasses flew off his nose. Kuzmenok hit him again and again.

The math teacher came in the classroom.

"What on earth? Break it up right now!" she screamed.

Kuzmenok silently sat down at the last desk. Kolya picked up his glasses. One lens was broken. Blood was flowing from the cut on his cheek.

"Kuzmenok, how did you get to be so stupid?" she yelled. "What if you had knocked his eye out? Klimov, go to the nurse right away."

"Are you going to tell Sergei when he comes home?" I asked Kolya. We were heading home. His cheek had a bandage stuck to it.

"Even if I don't tell him, my parents will still notice."

"Don't you want Sergei to beat him up?"

"He'll do it whether I want him to or not."

"You want to go skiing with me today?"

"No, I don't feel like it. I'm not in the mood."

My skis slid along on the trampled sidewalk snow. Two guys and a girl were standing by the last house on Motor Street right next to the railroad. They were all about twenty years old.

"Hey guy, I got a question for you," one yelled at me and blocked my path. The girl laughed. I didn't know her or the guys.

"Listen, I'll give you a hundred rubles if you do a little job for me," the guy laughed. He had pus-filled pimples on his cheeks. "Will you go up to this house and ask for Olya?"

"Why don't you go ask for her yourself?" said the girl. "You can keep going, kid."

"Don't listen to her. Do me a favor. Ask for her, huh?" said the guy. The other guy hugged the girl and they started kissing.

"Holy shit, have you two lost your fucking minds?" the pimply one yelled at them. "You're practically having sex in front of this little guy." All three of them cracked up. "Anyway, you'll go ask for me, yeah?"

I bent down, unlatched my bindings, took off my skis, opened the gate and went up to the door. An old motorcycle without its wheels was sitting by the shed. I knocked on the window.

"Who is it?" answered a man's voice.

"Is Olya there?"

"She ain't here anymore. She was off whoring around somewhere and bit the big one. Who the hell are you? Another one of her fuck buddies?"

Classes from the sixth through tenth grades were lined up along three walls of the gym. We were between sixth B and fifth A. The principal, the head of studies, and the military instructor were standing against the fourth wall. The principal Vassily Semenovich—short, snub-nosed, glasses, he also taught physics—put up his hand. Our head teacher pulled Kuzmenok by the back of the jacket when he was leaned forward and showed something to Sokol from A class.

"Dear children," said the principal. "We have gathered here today to hold an assembly in opposition to the American administration's plan to create a 'Star Wars' system, which is also called the 'Strategic Defense Initiative' or 'SDI'. Despite the fact that the word 'defense' is present in the title, this plan is nothing more than a new spin on the arms race, and we, together with every progressive society across the earthly sphere, must state our categorical opposition to the escalation of tensions and the arms race."

I was standing in the second row. Nikolaev was on one side of me; Kutepov was on the other. His blue jacket was speckled with dandruff and a scratch on his cheek had green ointment smeared on it. Kutepov looked at me and started to fall over. Kuzmenok was standing next to him. He took a step to the side, thinking Kutepov was goofing around. Kutepov fell all the way down, banging against the blackboard as he collapsed to the floor.

"What on earth, Kutepov?" The teacher bent over him, touched his shoulder, slapped his cheek. None of us were listening to the principal. Everybody was looking at Kutepov—six A and five B turned and looked too.

Kutepov opened his eyes.

"Are you alright?" asked the teacher. "Where are you hurt?"

"My head..."

"Go quickly to the nurse. Let's have a student monitor go with you. Be careful as you walk past everyone."

Kutepov got up slowly.

"Can you walk?" asked the teacher.

"I can."

Kutepov and Kovalenko walked on the bench by the wall to get to the exit. Some guys from eighth B grabbed their jackets as they went past. Their head teacher, Anna Sergeyevna shushed them and shook her fist at them.

"And now pupil Nikolai Osinovich from tenth A class, the chairman of our school's *Komsomol* committee, will give an address," said the principal.

The tenth grade classes were standing next to the parallel bars. Osinovich, a tall pimply guy in a skinny black fake leather tie and sneakers went up and stood beside the principal.

"On behalf of all the students in our school and on behalf of the *Komsomol* committee, I want to voice my protest against the government of the USA and its plans for the creation of 'Star Wars'. We want world peace. 'Star Wars' increases the likelihood of a new war and the outbreak of a new arms race."

I was sitting in the bedroom doing my algebra homework. Mama and Papa were having a conversation in the kitchen.

"What is he going to do now?" asked Papa. "Where will he live?"

"In a dormitory. He doesn't want to go live with Mama. He says he loves his independence."

"Exactly, independence," said Papa. "This whole thing with

59

Lena was all about his independence. He was only thinking of himself. He was buying records for a hundred rubles. Can you imagine doing such a thing?"

"First of all, it wasn't a hundred. It was seventy-five," said Mama. "And second, he didn't buy them with his regular wages— he got paid well for those expeditions in Uzbekistan every summer. And third, don't forget he was her second husband. And the first was some big head of something. She was spoiled, accustomed to luxury."

"What do you mean? What luxury? She's a decent woman and she took good care of us whenever we came over. They could have settled down and had children. Zhora is to blame for all of it. He shouldn't have drank so much..."

"Everybody else's cows are mooing, but you think yours are silent?" Mama yelled. "'He shouldn't have drank so much!' You recall how you came home the day before yesterday?"

"Semyonov's taking a leave of absence. We were giving him a send-off." Papa said.

"So if you're giving somebody a send-off that makes it okay to come home hammered?"

"Alright, this topic is closed," he said.

I stood up and went in the living room. Natasha was sitting on the couch. A pair of figure skaters was performing on the television screen. I closed the door. "Listen, what are they talking about?" I asked her.

"Uncle Zhora is divorcing Aunt Lena and moving into a dormitory."

"Why are they getting a divorce?"

Natasha shrugged her shoulders. "Ask him yourself if you

want."

"What, is it too hard for you to tell me or something?"

"I don't know, is all," she said. "They were having some kind of conflict. That and he was drinking."

"Why don't they have any children?"

"Don't ask people stupid question like that," she told me. "Don't ask them about it, alright? That's a personal question."

"So they're definitely getting a divorce? Or maybe they could still get back together?"

"I don't know," she said. "It seems pretty definite."

The figure skaters were bowing on the screen. The judges showed their scores. They all put up tens, except for one.

Kolya, Sergei, and I sat on the bed in their room and played Thousand. Sergei had grown his hair long and started listening to metal. His t-shirt had the letters "HMR" stenciled on it, which stood for "Heavy Metal Rock".

"So tell me, does he hassle everybody?" said Sergei. "This Kuzmenok, is he really tall for your class? Or really strong?"

"No, not really," I said. "Ignatovich is very strong. He knows judo. Kuzmenok doesn't mess with Ignatovich. He knows he'd beat him up."

"That means he's sly, but also brazen. I suspect he messed with somebody once and that guy didn't stand up to him. And everybody else just stood there and watched. So then he realized he could mess with everybody else, too. All of this is basic psychology. I'm not a fan of this personality type."

"Don't call it personality," interrupted Kolya. "He's a freak, it's not his personality."

"Can't you take a joke?"

"This isn't a joke. What if he'd knocked his eye out?" I said. "He hit him right in the glasses."

"You can't hit somebody in the glasses. That'll get him punched in the head. Where do you think we might find him?"

"Who the fuck knows," said Kolya. "Especially now that it's cold."

"Maybe he's playing hockey on the pond." I said.

"Do they have the rink flooded at your school?" Sergei asked.

"It is flooded but the guys don't play on that one."

"Then let's finish up this round and go for a walk. We'll find that idiot, okay? I pass. You?"

"Five." I said.

Kolya looked at his cards. "Ten."

"You go."

The start of the pond was behind the truck yard. Sometimes guys swam in it in the summer. I did too, twice last year. A spotlight from the truck yard illuminated a segment of ice. Six guys were playing, three on three. None of them had skates, the goalies didn't even have sticks. Their goal was pieces of brick laid out on the ice and the puck was a flattened tin can. I knew almost all the guys. They had finished eighth grade the year before and gone away to different vocational schools. Kuzmenok wasn't there. We walked along the truck yard's white brick wall and went out onto Chelyuskintsi. On the right by the Green Meadow trolley depot there were three trolleybuses. We turned at the five-story apartment building and walked past Bread and Milk on the ground floor of building #170-A.

"We could also check the bus stop," said Kolya. "Or over by building #101-B, across from the bookstore."

"We'll look everywhere," said Sergei. "We're on a hunt, which means we have to look high and low." He took out a pack of *Astras*, clicked his lighter and inhaled. "Freaks need to be punished," he said. "Kill them all!" he yelled in English. "That's from an Iron Maiden song."

Kuzmenok was sitting at the bus stop with Kosachenko and his little brother, who was in third grade.

"There he is," said Kolya.

"And the other two were not involved?" asked Sergei. Kolya nodded. "You're dismissed, men. We bid you farewell."

Kosachenko and his little brother got up and left. Sergei grabbed Kuzmenok by the collar. "And now we'll have a little talk with you," he said.

"I didn't touch him first. He started it," Kuzmenok said. "And I didn't mean to break his glasses. It was an accident."

Sergei punched Kuzmenok hard in the nose.

"Oops, that was an accident too," he said.

"No it's true, I didn't mean to. My word as a brother."

"Who exactly do you think is your brother here?" Sergei demanded. "You're a schmuck, not a brother. You got that? You only mess with ones who can't hit you back. It's true, isn't it? How about you mess with me? Hit me, huh? What if I don't hit you back? Maybe I'll forgive you if you prove you're not a pussy, huh? Hit me. Maybe you're not a pussy. Go ahead. Prove to me that you're not a pussy."

Kuzmenok lowered his head and looked at his boots.

"Well then, this is what I do with pussies."

Sergei got right into Kuzmenok's face and kneed him in the balls. Kuzmenok squatted down. Sergei punched him in the nose, in the jaw, then again in the nose.

"I hope you understand now that you can't hit guys that are weaker than you," said Sergei.

Kuzmenok nodded.

"If that's understood, then good. And if not, things are gonna get worse for you from here."

The sun burned low in the sky, not too bright. Everything was thawing. Classes were over for the day, and we were clearing the street. We had to scoop up the snow on the sidewalk with wooden shovels and throw it in the road.

Kuzmenok hurled some snow at the wheels of a *KamAZ* dump truck. His bruises had yellowed and were almost gone. Kolya and I didn't talk about any of it in class, and Kuzmenok himself told people that some guys from the Menzhinka neighborhood punched him in the face.

"What are you doing?" yelled the head teacher. "Did I not clearly explain to you that you must wait for vehicles to pass?"

"I won't do it anymore," said Kuzmenok.

The math teacher and our head teacher started talking. The

head teacher turned around. Kuzmenok threw snow at the wheels of a couple more dump trucks, first at a *ZIL* then some more at a *GAZ*. The rest of us started hurling snow at cars too. I took a whole shovelful and threw it at another dump truck, this one at an *Ural*.

An old sedan stopped with a screech of brakes. The driver jumped out of the car—a guy in a gray sweater and jacket. His rear window was all covered with snow. He charged at Kuzmenok.

"What are you doing, kid? You trying to get punched in the face?"

Kuzmenok threw down his shovel and ran away, the driver behind him. The head teacher and the math teacher turned around.

"What's this? What happened?" asked the head teacher.

"You need to keep a closer eye on your morons." The man said and stopped. Kuzmenok was already too far.

"You, sir, need to watch your mouth," she said.

"I don't take orders from you, got that? You're standing here flapping your lips and these fuckers are flinging snow at cars." He turned around and went back to his car.

"What a rude fellow. An ill-mannered boor," said the math teacher.

Two guys about sixteen years old were standing outside Emerald, the jewelry store.

"Hey, listen, come over here," said the tall and skinny one. "We need to talk to you."

"Which neighborhood are you from?" asked the other.

"Central," I said.

"What does that mean, Central?"

"There are three parts of town: Central, Lenin's, and October."

"Hang on, he's trying to stall us. Where do you live, what street?"

"Cheluskintsi."

"Whereabouts on Cheluskintsi?"

"Building #148. What's it to you?"

"What neighborhood is that?" the skinny one asked the other one.

"I don't know, either Worker's or Menzhinka. If he's Menzhinka he's one of us." He turned to me.

"What's your school?"

"17th."

"We're in the clear. That's Worker's."

The guys grabbed me and dragged me under an arch into a nearby courtyard. I tried to tear myself away. The skinny guy punched me in the nose. The blood flowed, dripping onto my jacket. A guy in a big fur cap was walking his dog in the courtyard. He looked at us and walked in the other direction.

"Alright, all the money you have, give it here," said the skinny one. "If I have to get it myself, things will get worse for you. You got that?"

I took a ten folded in half out of my pocket—Babushka had given it to me on the twenty-third of February, Soviet Army and Navy Day.

"That seems about right, yeah?" Skinny smiled.

"You're not holding out on us?" asked the other guy. "What if he's still got a hundred or something?"

The guys cracked up. I shook my head, bent down, picked

up some snow and wiped my nose. The guys disappeared into the depths of the courtyard.

"An absolute disgrace," said Mama. She and Papa were sitting in the kitchen eating potatoes.

"A juvenile is robbed downtown in broad daylight. Here's what I'd like to know—did any policemen see it happen or other people? Was anybody nearby?"

"There was some guy with a dog but he left right away," I said.

"If something like that had happened to one of his own kids he would have reacted differently," said Mama.

"Basically, you were the one who did the wrong thing," Papa said to me. "You should have assessed the situation right off the bat. What did you think, they wanted to ask you how to get to the library? If you see danger, don't second guess yourself, just run."

"What are you teaching him now?" said Mama. "The last thing we need is for him to run and fall under a car. It's so slippery on the road right now. A car's breaking distance is much longer than usual."

"Don't talk to me about breaking distance. I know about breaking distance without you telling me. But if you're going to take a stand you have to be able to defend yourself. Either that or you have to run away. I know what it's like. My first year at the institute I walked around with brass knuckles in my pocket. Back then you couldn't go anywhere without brass knuckles. An attack could pop out from behind any bush."

"Alright, that's enough. I can't listen to any more of this," said Mama. She shoved a potato onto her fork. The potato fell on the table and crumbled to pieces. "You can't ever teach him anything useful. Instead you run your mouth about a bunch of nonsense."

Mama gathered up the pieces of the potato on the table. I got up and went over to the window. Almost all the windows were lit up in Kindergarten #51 and Kindergarten #55, both on the other side of the courtyard. There were two paths to the kindergartens crisscrossing the courtyard. There were people walking on both of them.

I shook the snow off my skis, stood them in the corridor, and went into the main room, which was well heated. Babushka was sitting in an armchair by window. The radio was on in the next room. The dedications show was on: "And now we congratulate several folks on their eightieth birthdays."

"Well, how's the skiing?" asked Babushka.

"Like it always is."

"Sit for a spell?"

"Sure. Why are you so red? Were you crying? What for? Is it because of Uncle Zhora?"

"No, not because of him. It's just been such a life. Not a simple life. I was in the fourth grade when my father—your great-grandfather was exiled to Siberia. That was during the time of collectivization. Mama and I went with him. We survived seven years out there."

"Was he a kulak?" [18]

"What makes a man a kulak? He just worked, and the others drank and didn't do anything. Drinking, not doing anything, that was good, but work was bad. Sure, he employed workers. So what if he did? For that he was sent straight to Siberia? And I wasn't able to finish my studies, applied three times to Worker's Preparatory I did, but they didn't want to take the daughter of a kulak. They only took me after we returned from Siberia just before the war. Then I went straight to Worker's Preparatory thankfully, then the vocational institute. And then——."

"It's okay, Babushka. Please don't cry."

"Oh, I'm not going to cry. It's just been such a life. Vasya and I got to know each other, that was your grandpa. He was an orphan. I was the little daughter of a kulak. We got married and started our life, and then there it was, the war. Your grandpa went straight to the front, got injured right away, and then he was shell-shocked. That's why he died so early. You'll notice all the drunks, alcoholics, and lazy-bones are still alive, but our good man is not."

My grandfather died five years before. I didn't remember him very well. He was always sick. He spent a lot of time in the hospital. His left hand had deep scars left over from his shrapnel injury. Babushka later told me they wanted to amputate his hand but he wouldn't let them. Because of his ailment my grandfather was always very nervous, always cursing, and yelling at me for little things.

I was soldering fenders onto my Ferrari. At the neighboring table Pika was busy with his *BMW*, on the other side Shorty was tinkering with the acrylic paints. Rogovets wasn't there. An old guy in a trench coat with a briefcase had come to see him and they left together.

"Why doesn't anybody make new cord-track cars anymore?" I

asked Pika.

"What for? You know how many are still around from past years? There are plenty of cars to take to competition. But they still give Rogovets metal and money for motors and other stuff. And he keeps it all for himself. He's a crafty old crook but you wouldn't know it looking at him. He's got at least three jobs."

"Where else does he work?"

"All I know is that he works in a shoe repair shop."

"What does he do there?"

"What do you mean what does he do? He repairs shoes—glues them, resoles the heels. What else would he do?"

The door opened and Rogovets came in red in the face and smiling. He came up to the table and stopped behind my back.

"I'll tell you guys, I can't get to my pension soon enough!" he said, breathing vodka on me. "You know what I'm going to do when I'm on pension? Jack shit, that's what."

"What do you mean?" asked Pika.

"Don't play dumb with me. Haven't you ever seen the truck that takes the garbage away? And that guy who rides along with a shovel? He does jack shit. I once asked that guy, how much do you get paid? And he told me 'a hundred rubles to bring home to the old lady, plus another two hundred for myself.' So when I retire, I'll be doing jack shit. Unless fuckers like you drive me to an early grave. Alright, just kidding. Are we gonna win regionals this year?"

"Of course we'll win. That goes without saying," said Pika.

★

70

Mama and I were sitting on the couch watching the International Women's Day Concert. Papa was snoring in the bedroom. The lock clicked. Natasha peeked in the living room and looked at us in a weird way.

"Did you lock the front door?" asked Mama.

"Oh yeah, right, I'll get it right now..."

Natasha went back to the entry.

"Lock the second lock too, okay?"

"Yes, okay, okay. Just a minute."

Natasha messed around with the lock, came back in the room and sat in a chair with a big smile.

"Have you been drinking?" Mama asked.

"Well, yeah, but what's the big deal? My class gets together to celebrate the eighth of March, and I 'm not supposed to drink a glass of wine?" Natasha said.[19]

"Just one glass?"

"Well, two. But how exactly does one or two make a difference?"

"It's a very big difference. You're still only sixteen."

"In a month I'll be seventeen."

"You're still just sixteen and you're a girl. Is that normal to you? Drinking alcohol, coming home tipsy. Should a young girl really be carrying on like this?"

"What does all that mean anyway? I don't understand why everybody says that, like alcohol is so bad. You, the teachers at school, a bunch of old guys on television..."

"You're trying to say that alcohol is a good thing? You think this is normal? A sixteen-year-old girl coming home drunk? Alcoholism is normal in your opinion?

"Not everybody who drinks is an alcoholic. Papa drinks too

and comes home drunk but he's not an alcoholic, right? Or are you saying he is an alcoholic?"

"Don't compare yourself to him," Mama said. "He's a man. Men drink more."

"Men can drink, but women aren't allowed to, right?" Natasha said. "And you say we've got equal rights."

"Alright, we're finished with this conversation. Go wash up and get to bed. You have school tomorrow. And please think about the consequences of your behavior. What kind of example are you setting for your brother?" Mama looked at me. I turned away. "Don't think he doesn't notice anything. Don't you see all the alcoholics around here? They're hanging around outside the beer hall all the time. You think he doesn't see them?"

Mama waved her hand and turned back to the television. Natasha got up, left the living room, and slammed the door. A crazy-looking long-haired singer named Valery Leontyev came on the screen in a sparkly blue costume.

"The Soviet nation has suffered a great loss," said the announcer on the radio. "The General Secretary of the Central Committee of the Communist Party of the Soviet Union, Konstantin Utinovich Chernenko, has passed away in his seventy-fifth year."

"They're dropping like flies," said Papa.

Mama looked at him. "Don't say such things. No more of that."

"No more of what? Why are you so scared of everything? Just

like your mama. For her it makes sense, she remembers the old days. And furthermore, it's not like I said anything bad. I just told it like it is. He was the third general secretary in two and half years, less than that even. How exactly am I wrong?"

Mama didn't answer. I picked up my plate and got up from the table.

"Thanks for dinner," I said.

"My pleasure," said Mama.

"Did you do your homework already?" asked Papa.

I nodded.

"What's with you lately?" Mama looked at Papa. "You never show any interest." Papa shrugged. Tedious music was playing on the radio.

During our first class—Algebra—the head teacher came in. The math teacher stood up and went over to the window.

"You all of course must have heard about what happened yesterday," said the head teacher. "This is a huge loss and the entire Soviet nation is in mourning. But we cannot let down our guard during this time because our enemies don't rest. They will be eager to utilize this opportunity for all sorts of provocations, specifically aggressive actions against our country. Tomorrow on the day of the funeral for Konstantine Ustinovich we will not have school."

"Yahoo! A day off!" yelled Kuzmenok.

"Sergei, that's enough. First of all it's not a day off, it's just a non-school day. And second, it's downright blasphemous to be happy when our entire nation is suffering from such great sorrow.

I want you all to understand this. Tomorrow may be a day without classes but I advise you to stay home, don't ride or walk anywhere because as I already told you, in the event of a provocation from an enemy state it is entirely possible that we may have an evacuation."

"What does that mean?" asked Nevedomtseva.

"It means that in the event of any danger, certain portions of the population such as children and elderly people may be taken out of the city on special trains."

"Where will we go?" Nevedomtseva asked.

"You, Lena need to listen before you ask questions, alright? I'm trying to explain to you that an evacuation is theoretically possible but that doesn't mean that it will occur. It's just necessary that you know about this and are prepared, so that you are not caught unaware in the event of an evacuation. And now I need to take four boys and four girls for an honor guard at the memorial assembly. So, whose shirt is clean?"

A portrait of Chernenko drawn in charcoal was sitting on a table by the gymnasium wall. One corner of it was wrapped in a black ribbon. I was standing on the left side of the portrait. Lozovskaya was on the right. We were giving the Pioneer's salute. Classes from fifth through tenth grade stood along the other three walls. In the middle of the gym the principal was giving a speech:

"On this day, a day that is so difficult for the entire Soviet nation, your objective must still be the following: to study and gather knowledge, because it's in knowledge that you will find strength. And it is this very strength that will enable you to defend our homeland from its enemies and to achieve the utmost success in the battle for our primary goal, which is the continuous construction of our communist society."

My right arm was numb, I could barely hold it up. I didn't know how much time was left before the changing of the guard. I began to move my hand slowly to the right, then the left. That made it a little easier.

The assembly was over. The students were pushing each other around as they left the gym. Someone giggled loudly. The head teacher rushed over to me. "Were you trying to disgrace me in front of the whole school? What was wrong with your salute? Why was your hand going back and forth like that?"

"My arm hurt. I couldn't keep holding it up like that and I didn't know how long until the change."

"Well, that's the last time you get to do this sort of assignment for me."

The table was pulled out into the center of the room and covered with a yellow tablecloth that had transparent red flower stickers on it, which were supposed to look festive. Natasha, Kolya, Mama, Papa, Babushka, Uncle Zhora, and I were all at the table. Papa poured vodka for himself and Uncle Zhora, wine for Natasha, Mama, and Babushka, and lemonade for Kolya and me.

"Well then, shall we drink again to Igor?" asked Babushka. "My wish for you, my grandson, is the best of everything." Everyone turned and looked at me.

"Hang on, let's take a picture," I said.

On the magazine table, next to the plate of bread slices—there wasn't room for it on the big table—sat my *Smena* camera and *Chaika* flash. The flash was a present from my parents for my birthday. I attached it to the camera, set the F-stop and exposure, and then looked in the viewfinder.

"Attention everyone, I'm taking a picture!" The shutter clicked and the flash went off.

"Now, how about I take a shot so you can be in the picture," said Papa.

He put his wine glass down on the table and took the camera from me. I sat in his spot between Kolya and Uncle Zhora.

"Everybody ready? Watch the birdie—"

I squinted during the flash and probably blinked.

"I propose that we drink this third toast not only to the birthday boy Igor but also to his parents," said Uncle Zhora.

Everybody clinked each other's glasses. When he clinked with me, Uncle Zhora spilled a little vodka on the plate of Russian salad.

I took a gulp of lemonade, put down the glass, and took some cucumbers with sour cream from the salad dish. These were the first cucumbers of the year.

"When it was announced about Chernenko, I was talking to Ushakov from the accounting department," said Papa. "And he said there's one guy in the Politburo named Gorbachev who was fifty-four years old, but he'd never be appointed. And then—surprise, surprise—Gorbachev got the job. No, I consider this a good thing because if they would have appointed some old guy again—"

"That doesn't matter. It doesn't matter who they appointed, everything will stay the same," said Uncle Zhora.

"Why?" Natasha looked at him, serious.

"Because, Natalya, the problems in this country are too dire, we need extreme changes, true reforms."

"Like the school reforms?" asked Natasha. "Honestly, I haven't noticed any improvements."

"I notice them," said Uncle Zhora. "They increased my salary for the head teacher position."

"Me too. I'm getting more for grading notebooks," said Mama. "Thirty rubles a month. You were talking about larger problems, and I agree with you. There are indeed many problems. But how do we solve them? For example, how do you combat drunkenness?"

"Drunkenness isn't that big of a problem," said Uncle Zhora, gnawing on a chicken leg. "A much more serious problem is on the horizon, and that's drug addiction. But nobody's talking about it even though it's already here. For three years in a row I've gone on those expeditions in Central Asia. I've seen the poppy fields there. And I've seen the people who go out there for the poppy sticks. They're in nice *Volgas*, they're wearing suits. They have gold teeth."

"What do you mean? Is poppy a drug?" I asked. "Is it like that when it's on bagels too?"

"No, not like that," said Uncle Zhora. "Bagels have poppy seeds, this comes from poppy sticks."

"Alright, that's enough of you filling the children's heads with your sticks," said Papa. "It's a little early for them to know about that stuff."

"So you think if they don't know about this, it won't be a threat to them?" said Uncle Zhora.

"I don't think anything."

"Or, maybe you think drug addiction doesn't really exist in

the Union?"

"Take some herring salad, who hasn't had any yet?" said Mama.

"We can go in the other room. We'll come back for dessert, okay?" I whispered to Kolya.

A black box with a *Chaika GAZ-13* model car sat in the bedroom on my table—it was my gift from Uncle Zhora. I carefully opened the box, took out the model and set it on the table, then opened the doors and the trunk.

"Why doesn't the hood open?" asked Kolya.

"I don't know."

"I think I know. Look, it says here in a foreign language: 'Collection Model'. That means they make it to sell abroad for export, but the motor in the *Chaika* is secret and foreigners aren't allowed to know what kind it is and how it's built."

"Maybe."

"Which model do you want to get next?"

"A *Niva*."

In the living room, the voices of Uncle Zhora and Papa were getting louder.

"They could have dropped two bombs on Cuba and that would have been it," said Uncle Zhora. "But the Americans decided against the idea. They said, 'You want Cuba? Here you go, you guys can go ahead and feed it.'"

"If they'd have dropped those bombs it would have started a war," said Papa.

"It wouldn't have started anything," said Uncle Zhora.

"I'm telling you, it would have."

"You don't understand all the complexities. You sit in your

engineering bureau and can't see anything past your own nose."

"Like you see so much at your school. You're my hero."

"I'm so sick of listening to you." The legs of a chair rustled on the carpeted path. "That's enough for me."

"Settle down, Zhora," said Babushka.

"Let him go!" yelled Papa. "I'm sick of listening to him, too. All he does is wait around the whole night thinking of things to bug me about."

"You wait around for the very same thing, don't you see?" Uncle Zhora yelled back. "You know what you are? A simple-minded oaf, that's what!"

The living room door opened and Uncle Zhora went to the entryway.

"Go bring him back," said Mama. "You don't need to spoil a kid's party."

"The kid wasn't even here to hear it," said Papa. "Let him go. I don't want to look at him anymore."

I rang the bell. Kolya opened the door.

"Hi," I said. "Want to go with me to the movies at the Motherland?"

"Which movie?"

"*Chingachguk, the Big Snake*. It's about Indians."

"No, I don't think I'll go," he said. "There's a show on TV. It's called *Visitor From the Future*. The first episode was on yesterday. Did you see it?"

"I didn't see it. So you're just going to sit at home the whole vacation?"

"Who said I'm staying home the whole time? I'm just going to watch a show. Come back over tonight, alright?"

"Alright. Bye," I said.

I walked out of the building's front entry. The snow in the court-yard had almost melted. There were only a few dirty, blackened patches of snow next to the building.

Two guys from tenth were standing at the Worker's bus stop. I knew their nicknames, Baron and Adolph. Adolph was in an almost new pair of jeans—just a little worn in the front. Baron was in some regular gray pants. Both were smoking.

A trolleybus pulled up. I got on. Adolph and Baron stayed at the bus stop. I sat in the tall seat over one of the wheels.

Two young teachers from School #17 got on at Motor Street and sat in the seat ahead of me. One taught mathematics, the other Russian language, but neither of them was mine, they taught other classes. The math teacher was talking.

"So she looked at me like I was a fool. And then she started lecturing me: we're not allowed to give too many twos, because what would the district say? Our school has a bad reputation, our neighborhood isn't very good, we need to compete with the good schools. So then I told her, 'it's like we don't have a five point system anymore, it's a three point system now isn't that right?' She was quiet for a second then she stood her ground again. No, that bothers me even more. We have standards for assigning grades, I re-read them myself not long ago. A two is the score for an incorrect answer, and if the answer is absent then it gets a one."

"If everyone observed the standards half the pupils in our school would have a two." Said the Russian teacher.

"Well, not half but at least a quarter, you're exactly right. Here's what I think you're saying: if somebody isn't capable of studying in a normal school, then let him get sent off to one of the 'special' schools, we don't need him rattling the teachers' nerves and preventing the other students from learning. And if he is capable but doesn't want to learn, then let us give him a two for the quarter and he has to repeat the year. Maybe that would teach him something."

"Absolutely. I'm so sick of all of this hogwash. The threes are a farce and our honor students are a farce too. Honor students get straight fives but all they have is just enough knowledge to get into the mechanical engineering institute or best case scenario the pedagogical institute."

"But they don't even need to be an honor student for that. I have a cousin who goes to School #24. He's probably a three-to-four student and he's going into the mechanical engineering institute next year in the computer science department. It's a very good specialty."

The trolleybus stopped by the Kubsheva factory employee's club. That was where Worker's ended and the Menzhinka neighborhood started. Behind the employee's club was the factory's stadium, Vocational School #70 and its dorms, and closer to Worker's were the forking streets of Cheluskintsi and Cosmonaut. In third grade I saw the movie *Warlords of Atlantis* at the employees' club. Guys from Worker's and Menzhinka took up almost half the hall. Back then I still didn't know that Menzhinka and Worker's were enemies. Everybody sat together and nobody got into it with anybody else, in large part because that movie was really scary. The scariest part of all was when some kind of snake pushed its head inside their glass-bottom submersible. They stuck an electric cable in its mouth and it croaked.

★

Our charter bus went past the green grocer and the department store, my building, and building #150. I had asked Rogovets earlier if I could be picked up outside my building but he said, "What if you're running late? I'll have to run around looking for you? This is a competition, not just any old trip. You show up at three o'clock at the school like everybody else and we'll leave from there."

Rogovets and six guys from the club including me were sitting on the bus, plus a guy from the school district and a reporter from the *Mogilev Pravda* with a photographer.

"Why are you competing in Bobruisk instead of Mogilev?" the journalist asked Rogovets.

"Mogilev doesn't have a cord car racetrack."

"They have one in Bobruisk?"

"They do. Bobruisk is a city of Jews and those Jews make sure they have everything!" Rogovets smirked. "Well, what they have isn't exactly a cord track but there's a dance platform in the park, they converted it and we've competed there for five years. But don't you gents try and tell me it's beneath you to travel with us to Bobruisk. You're on the clock, you get paid extra for trips and you even get food vouchers for business travel."

"You're right of course, that's a good point," said the reporter.

"Where are we spending the night?" asked the photographer.

"First class accommodations at the Hotel Bobruisk."

"You know, I've seen this place you're calling first class. But there's nothing better in that city."

"As a matter of fact," said Rogovets. "We're only staying there because you're going with us. Last year we spent the night at some kind of sports school, all in one room, both the trainers and the guys."

"So that means a whole bottle for two of us." The journalist winked at Rogovets. He unbuttoned his jacket and took it off, which left him in a gray vest with a black *Adidas* crown, and a red scarf around his neck.

The city came to an end. The bus drove onto the gray asphalt. Out the window, the brown fields and bare black trees grew smaller. From time to time oncoming cars drove past. The sky was gray, covered with storm clouds.

The Hotel Bobruisk was right in the city center across from Lenin Square. I was sharing a room with Pika. Rogovets, the guy from the district, and the journalist and photographer were staying in the neighboring rooms, also two-bed. The rest of the guys were staying as a big group in a five-bed on the second floor. I stepped out on the balcony and looked down on the street at the cars and trolleybuses, then at the windows of a big gray apartment building opposite our hotel. The windows were unusually close. A lady in a blue bathrobe was taking something out of her refrigerator. A guy in sweatpants and a t-shirt was watching television.

I went back in the room. It had two beds, two night stands, a magazine table with an old television, and two armchairs exactly like the ones we used to have at home: deep green with wooden legs. My parents had bought a new living room set a year before, and a guy from Papa's design office paid him a very low price and took the old armchairs, the couch, and a little table for his dacha.

Pika turned on the television. One station worked but not very well and almost without any sound. Pika twisted the antenna but everything stayed the same. He turned off the television.

"Why does every city have a hotel named after the city?" I asked. "In Mogilev there's Hotel Mogilev, in Minsk there's Hotel Minsk. Here it's Hotel Bobruisk."

"That's so you don't forget which city you're in. Alright, I'm out of here. I have some friends here. I'll leave the key with you. When I get back I'll knock. So you can open up for me, got it? And don't you dare not open it for me. Alright, I'm off."

Pika put on his jacket and left. I went over to the window. The guy was still watching television, but the lady wasn't in her kitchen anymore. In another apartment an old man with a gray beard and long gray hair was standing by the window.

I knocked on the door of the guys' room and went in.

"You bring your pillow?" asked Goose. "We don't have any extras."

"What's the pillow for?"

"What do you mean, what's it for? We're gonna have a pillow fight. Quick, let's go to your room."

"Let the games begin!" yelled Goose.

He swung his pillow at Dodik and hit his shoulder. Somebody hit me on the head and everything went black for a second. I almost fell but grabbed the headboard on the bed. Goose jumped on the bed and hit Dodik down below him—blocking him from getting up on the bed too. Shorty swung at Greenie. I ran up behind Shorty, swung hard, and hit him in the head. Shorty crashed down on the bed. Greenie pounded him two times then turned on me. Shorty got up to help him.

The guys were lying on their beds. I was sitting on the chair across from the washstand. Feathers from the pillows were scattered all over the floor. Water was dripping from the faucet.

"I fucking knocked you out, huh, Shorty?" asked Greenie. "Like in that movie *The Stunt Man*. Who saw it last year?"

"I saw it," said Dodik. "There were naked babes in it."

"Well yeah, there were, but it was hard to see them. They were at a distance."

"You know a good place to look for naked babes?" said Shorty. "The swimming pool."

The guys laughed.

"They have bathing suits on there," I said.

"True, kid," said Greenie. "You're still a little young to be looking at babes. Only in bathing suits for you and Shorty."

"You morons," said Shorty. "Of course they're in bathing suits. But you guys know what the swimmers do? When the coach leaves they pick one babe and push her into a corner. Then the swimmers strip the chick and feel her up. And you can see everything except her pussy. They never take off her bikini bottom, they're too scared."

"You can go ahead and tell the kid your stories," said Dodik.

85

"But I've been in that pool a hundred times and I never saw anything like that. You jerk off too much Shorty, that's why you think there's naked babes everywhere."

"You're the one who's always jerking off," said Shorty.

"I don't get it, you guys," said Dodik. "I asked him point-blank but he didn't want to admit it. Do you jerk off or not, huh? This one's a kid, maybe he really doesn't jerk off yet. I would believe him because he's still a kid and they don't always jerk off."

"Alright, quit fucking with Shorty," said Greenie. "Maybe he's got a huge one and he already stuck it in somebody. How long is it, Shorty? Three centimeters?"

Shorty turned toward the wall and covered his head with a pillow.

I got up. "Well, I'm gonna go."

"Are you gonna go jerk off?" asked Dodik. The guys giggled. "A man is known by the company he keeps." He nodded at Shorty. "You'd better jerk off Shorty, so you'll be in good shape for the competition tomorrow and all."

"Our competition continues with the electromobile category!" the head judge announced into the microphone. "At the starting line we have contestant Igor Razov from the city of Mogilev, member of the Citywide Office of Youth Engineers Model Car Club."

I took my truck, an old fashioned *GAZ-51* pick-up, and went to the open gate in the chain-link fence around the dance square. The judges were sitting at a table in front of the gate. I took my

GAZ to the cord track, hooked it up to the cord and flipped the switch. The car took off. I put my hand up for the judges to begin recording the time. The photographer came up to the open gate and focused his lens on me.

★

Our charter bus drove past the sign with "BOBRUISK" crossed out as we left the city.

"Alright guys, for the first time all year I'm not gonna bust your chops," said Rogovets. "Because you were great today!"

Out of the six of us, four including me took first place in our categories. Shorty was the only one who choked. He couldn't get his race model to push off the starting block. And Goose didn't even compete—his racecar had something wrong with its motor. Everyone who took first place got red ribbons with "Regional Youth Champion" on them and the "valuable prizes" were *Smena* cameras. I didn't know what I was going to do with another *Smena*.

"Hey chief, let's stop!" Rogovets yelled at the driver. The bus drove onto the side of the road. "Okay, now guys, get out and go to the toilet, alright? We've still got a long road ahead of us and there won't be any more stops."

The guys got off the bus. I stayed in my seat.

"What about you?" Rogovets asked me.

"I don't want to."

"What do you mean, you don't want to? Don't play dumb with me. Come on, let's get out and get some fresh air." He pushed me toward the door.

"Don't you know anything, kid?" Pika said to me. He was smoking, hiding his pack of *Stolichnies* and matches in his pocket. "The men need to hit the bottle and they don't want to do it in front of you."

We walked around the bus. Shorty wrote with his finger on its dirty backside: "Citywide Young Engineers—Champions." The rest were pissing in the roadside bushes.

"They gave you first place to be nice," said Shorty. "Your car was very simple. You know what Rogovets told me? He said, 'Any moron could flick the switch on that car.'"

I punched Shorty in the nose with all my strength. He staggered, stepping backward toward the bus. Then I kicked him in the balls. Shorty doubled over crying.

"Check it out! The kid beat up Shorty!" Pika said, thrusting his hand at me. "Gimme five!"

Shorty straightened up and wiped the snot from his hands. A new *MAZ* big rig with *SOVTRANSPORT* on its trailer drove by on the highway. Behind him was a police car and a black *Chaika* limousine.

"Slyunkov must be going to Mogilev, you think?" said Pika. "That motherfucker."[20]

We walked into the cemetery. There wasn't a fence around it. Wrought iron grave borders and crosses were sticking out of the ground behind the trees.

"That house over there used to be ours." Babushka pointed toward the edge of the forest. It was about fifty meters away. "We lived in it until Papa was pronounced a kulak and exiled."

"Who lives there now?" asked Natasha.

"I don't know. Some people. It's none of my business."

"Didn't you try to do anything? So you could go back?"

"What for? We built our house after the war. Your grandpa was a veteran of the war, so he was able to get timber for the wood."

Babushka took a red egg leftover from Easter and moved it around on the grave three times like she was making the sign of the cross. She made the dye for the eggs herself using onion peels. Today was *Radonitsa*, the ninth day after Easter, a day for remembering those who had passed. There were people sitting around almost every grave.

"Sleep peacefully, Vasenka, let the earth be your feather bed," Babushka said, crying. Mama put her arms around Babushka.

Mama, Papa, Natasha, and I squatted down around grandfather's grave. Babushka laid newspaper over the grave and put down a plate full of food. Papa opened the bottles of vodka and lemonade.

"Well, let's remember him," said Babushka.

We drank. Papa and Babushka had vodka, the rest of us lemonade. I took a fat piece of *blin*[21] with butter and had a bite.

A drunk guy came over and leaned on our fence. He looked at Babushka.

"Hi Ivanovna!"

"Hello," Babushka answered and turned away.

The guy got up and left.

"He's one of the local drunks," said Babushka. "He wanted me to pour him a glass."

There was a table inside the border of a neighboring grave with about twenty people sitting at it. Some guy was singing:

Two ducks flew
Two geese too...

"Are you out of your fucking mind, Semyon? Dancing on somebody's grave?" Somebody interrupted him. The guy went silent.

★

"Everybody ready!" cried the military instructor. "Forward
march."

The formations from other schools began to move up ahead of
us. Our instructor went up to the instructor of #28, also a major
but in artillery instead of tank forces. They something said to each
other. Our instructor returned.

"As you were!" he yelled. "We're on in ten minutes. The cere-
monial meeting still isn't over."

We were standing beside Lenin Square across from the
Nature's Gifts store—guys from the sixth and seventh grades from
all the schools in the neighborhood. We had come here to rehearse
three times before Victory Day.[22] At first the instructor said they
would give us special uniforms and flags that said "40 Years of
Victory" but then they forgot about that part. They said to show
up in our school uniforms with white shirts and black boots. Any
boots actually, but preferably black. Kuzmenok turned his back
on Kirillov, almost leaning against him, and elbowed him hard in
the stomach. Kirillov sat down and cried, then ran away from the
formation.

"What's going on here?" yelled the instructor. "What's the

matter? Where the hell is he going? Well, run him down quickly! Not everybody, no, three should be enough."

Kuzmenok, Nikolaev, and Strelchenko caught up with Kirillov by the entrance of Nature's Gifts and grabbed him by the jacket. He resisted. Kuzmenok punched him in stomach a couple times, not too hard. The guys from the other schools turned and looked.

"Bring him over here!" yelled the instructor.

Kirillov was brought forward. His face was red with tears.

"What happened? You can tell me, what happened?" asked the instructor, repositioning his glasses.

Kirillov was silent.

"Well, get back in line quickly, and if this happens one more time I'll give you a zero in conduct for the year. Understood?"

Kirillov nodded. Kuzmenok poked him in the side with his fist.

Up ahead someone yelled, "Everybody ready!"

"Everybody fall in, on the double!" said the instructor. "Ready!" The formation from #28 was already advancing forward. "Quick march!"

We went out onto the square. Girls from our school and the others were in their white aprons, holding hands on both sides of the square. There were veterans on the platform in military and civilian garb with decorations and medals. Someone's voice spoke into the microphone:

"Today on this day that is so special for our entire country—the fortieth anniversary of our victory in the Great Patriotic War—we can assure our veterans that they can put their trust in this young generation. We see before us several formations of pupils from schools in the Central district who have come here today on this day of remembrance to pay their respects to all those who were killed in the war and to honor our veterans. They say thank you, for your heroism on the front and diligent work in the rear, to all of you who have gathered on this day—our day of victory!"

Our formation turned onto First of May and stopped.

"Alright everyone, your assignment is complete," said the instructor. "You may head home but don't rush right off. Remember to exhibit discipline—"

Nobody was listening to him. The guys from our formation scampered every which way in a flurry of blue uniforms, white shirts, and red ties.

The swallows were screeching as they flew over the courtyard. Chestnut branches with fresh green leaves were stirring outside the kitchen window. Sergeyev, a guy who lived on the other side of our building was driving past in his invalid car. He had his leg amputated in the war and walked with a prosthetic, leaning on a cane. Every year on the ninth of May he wore his war uniform with medals and red star decorations.

I took a bottle of cream from the refrigerator, pressed my thumb through the yellow foil, peeled it off and poured some cream in a glass. I opened the pantry, took out a new packet of tea cookies and a jar of strawberry jam that Mama had made the year before with berries from Babushka's kitchen garden. The lock clicked in the entryway.

Natasha said to somebody, "Come in. My parents aren't home,

just my brother."

She glanced in from the entryway. "Hi," she said.

"Hi," I answered, munching on a cookie.

Natasha had a guy with her. I recognized him. He had gone to School #17 like us. He graduated a year or two ago.

He nodded at me.

"Hi. I'm Lesha."

"Igor."

He nodded again. I took another cookie from the pack. Natasha and Lesha went in the living room. They closed the door behind them. In the door, in place of the glass window, there was a sheet of white, opaque plexiglass. I knocked the glass out when I was four years old. I was running from the bedroom to the living room and the door was locked from the inside. Natasha was doing her homework and she didn't want me getting in her way. I took a running jump and hit the door with my fists. The glass shattered and the shards cut my hand. My parents weren't home and Natasha bandaged my hand. I cried, and she gave me her sweet cream ice cream from the freezer.

The front door closed and the lock clicked. Natasha came in from the entryway. I got up from behind the table. "Have you been going out with him for very long?" I asked.

"A week."

"How did you meet him?"

"We knew each other a long time ago. He went to 17th too."

"I remember him."

"I was in eighth, he was in tenth. We ran into each other on the trolleybus not long ago. I was going to my class at the labor training center and he was coming from the institute. He's studying to be a mechanical engineer. Do you not like him?"

"No, no, he's fine, he's a brother," I said.

"A brother, you say. You're the one who's 'one of the brothers.' He's an adult already. He's independent."

"Can I tell our parents about him?"

"If you want. I'm a grown woman. I can get together with whoever I want," Natasha said.

I went back to the table and looked out the window. On the clothesline by the building's gas tanks, Nizovtsova from the fifth floor was hanging some laundry: enormous ladies bloomers, blue and pink.

"Check," said Kuzmenok.

I pushed my king one cell to the right. The board and its pieces were on the landing between the second and third floors. Our class was on duty at school, and Kuzmenok asked to be on hall monitor duty with me. His mama gave him a chess set for his birthday, but out of our whole class only he and I knew how to play. Uncle Zhora taught me how two years before. I don't know where Kuzmenok learned.

"Check again," Kuzmenok moved his bishop. "Hey kid, where are you running? Come back down here and try that again!"

The kid turned around, came back down the stairwell, and walked back up slowly. Kuzmenok kicked him in the butt—not hard, just as a "prophylactic measure." I took out his bishop with my knight.

"Wait, I didn't see that." said Kuzmenok. "I get a do-over, okay?"

"Okay, you can have a do-over. Go ahead."

Andron from seventh B, the toughest from his class in a fight, came out of the buffet with shortbread in his hand.

"You're not too shitty a chess player, huh Kuzya?" he said.

"What's your point?" said Kuzmenok.

"I didn't catch that. What was that you said to me?"

"What's the problem with what I said?"

"You're a real smart ass, aren't you?"

"Get out of here, don't interrupt our game." Kuzmenok picked up his bishop and moved it two cells on a diagonal.

Andron knocked the board with his foot. The pieces flew off onto the landing, and Andron busted up laughing and broke off a piece of his shortbread. Kuzmenok punched him in the nose. The piece of shortbread fell on the floor and crumbled. I pressed myself into the corner by the radiator. Andron hit him and kicked him at the same time. Kuzmenok tumbled down the steps. The glass in the hallway door reverberated when he crashed into it. Kuzmenok touched the side of his head and looked at his fingers, which had blood on them. Andron went down the steps, back to Kuzmenok, and raised his fist. Kuzmenok flinched. Andron smiled.

"Eight kopecks for the shortbread."

Kuzmenok reached in his pocket, took out some change, and started counting. Andron took it all.

We started a new game. Kuzmenok's head was bandaged.

"You think I'm not gonna get him back?" said Kuzmenok. "I'll get him back. Damn straight I will. I'll get him back this summer.

95

He'll be on his knees, begging for forgiveness. What, you don't believe me? I'm gonna bring you along so you'll be with me to see him begging for forgiveness, you got that?"

"Got it. Your move."

"But you were watching, right? He's stronger than me, but I didn't piss myself when he fucked with me. Right? Check."

The bell rang three times. The intercom came on: "Attention! All teachers are summoned for a meeting!"

"Fuck yeah, there won't be any Algebra, huh?" said Kuzmenok.

"Why won't there be? Maybe it'll only be five or ten minutes."

"I'm telling you it'll be at least half an hour, maybe the whole lesson. Anyway, let's finish the game, and then I'm going home."

Kids were rushing down the hall on the first floor. I went out on the steps. There were guys from ninth and tenth smoking out there.

The apple trees were flowering in the courtyard. The grass was covered with white petals. Behind the trees a guy and a babe from tenth were chatting about something. She giggled.

Someone hollered inside the school:

"Don't throw out my briefcase! Are you a total moron?"

A brown briefcase fell from a window on the third floor, plopped down on the playground and opened up. Some notebooks fell out of it.

Our train was passing by a hill. Some guys were burning a bonfire on it. Their bikes were lying beside them. There was a guy who looked about Papa's age with us in the compartment. The fourth spot was free. The guy took a bottle of *Zhigulevskoye*[23] out of his bag and hooked it on the bottle opener under the table.

"Want some beer?" he asked Papa. "I can get an extra glass from the conductor."

"No thanks," Papa said.

"I just love a good brew. I have to say, Mogilev has some very good beer. And not just bottled, on tap, too. I didn't care for this one at first, but then I tried it in another city when I was on business. My name is Zhenya. And you are?"

"Petya. And this is my youngest, Igor."

"Are you visiting family?"

"No, I'm on business. I'm taking him with me to show him Moscow."

"I'm going to see my son. He's serving in the army in Kaluga. He's an exemplary fellow, a very good young man. He was all into weightlifting and then, would you believe it, he snuck away to the tech school—cold storage and equipment. When he finished he went off to the army. And everything's going well for him there. You know, he's an athletic fellow. His health is good, it's just his eyesight he ruined when he was little reading under the blanket with a flashlight." The guy took a big swig of beer. "I really need to tell you something. Here's the thing—sometimes I snore in the night. You'll have to say, 'Zhenya, stop snoring.' And you can touch my shoulder, okay?"

Papa nodded.

The escalator was creeping downward. I was holding the plastic railing and watching the passengers on the neighboring escalator. They were going up. The white lamps were flashing past.

"Which station are we going to?" I asked.

"Polezhaevskaya. At first we'll go to Gorkovskaya, and from there we'll transfer to Pushkinskaya."

"Are you going to be a long time at the institute?"

"I told you already, I'll do my best to get it all done quickly."

"Hey, maybe you could let me go to Red Square by myself?"

"No. And there will be no further discussion about that," he said. "You'll sit and wait downstairs. Read your book. Okay?"

"Okay," I said.

There was an abstract design made from pieces of metal pipe on the wall of the lobby. A security lady was sitting in the windowed booth. A guy with a beard, a briefcase, and wearing worn jeans went up to the booth and said something. She looked at him. The guy went through the revolving door to the elevator. I opened my book, *School* by Arkady Gaidar.[24] It was on the summer reading list.

The chimes on the clock tower began to sound.

"This is so weird," I said to Papa. "I can't believe I'm in Red

Square. I've seen it so many times on television."

"Does the real thing look different?"

"No, it's just kind of weird. Don't you think it's weird??"

"I've seen it lots of times before."

A black *Volga* drove up to the gates of Spasskaya Tower at the Kremlin and stopped. The gates opened and the car went in.

"Who could that be?" I asked.

"I don't know, maybe some minister. Or a deputy."

"Does Gorbachev come here, too?"

"Probably."

I took out my *Smena*, snapped some pictures of Spasskaya Tower, the mausoleum, a section of the battlement walls and the church just outside the square.

We walked up close to the church. Papa stood with the memorial as his background as I snapped his picture. The memorial was inscribed in old Russian: "To citizen Minin and Prince Pozharsky from a grateful Russia. 1818." I didn't really understand what it meant.

The little tables at the café were right on the street. Over the kitchen in the corner there was smoke from the shashlik on the grill.[25] A Georgian waiter came over to us. He was a fat guy with a gray mustache and whiskers.

"Two orders of shashlik, a pint of beer, a small carafe of vodka, and a bottle of Fanta," said Papa. The waiter left.

"He probably makes more in one day here than I make in a month."

"How do you know?"

"Beer and shashlik are always very profitable. A guy can make more money on those than anything else. Especially right next to the Exhibition Center like this. Anyway, we're not here to talk about that. What really matters is that you're here, that you get to see the capital. If Natashka wasn't taking her exams I would have brought her too. She's never been to Moscow either."

I took the bottle of Fanta and poured it in a glass. Papa held up his glass of vodka.

"Well, lets drink to Moscow, to you and me in the capital, to the best city ever. 'My song drifts, my heart sings these words about you, Mosco-o-o-w,' he sang.

We clinked glasses. Papa tossed back his vodka in one swig, drank some beer, and took a piece of shashlik with his fork. I took a drink of my Fanta.

Papa chewed his shashlik and said, "Little Igor, you shouldn't look at me like that just because I'm drinking vodka. Everybody has his own quota for how much he has to drink in his life. You know, they say that when a man is born a star appears in the sky. And on it, on the star, there's a barrel, and that barrel is what he has to drink throughout his life. If somebody has a big barrel, he has to drink a lot. For some guys it's small, and then it's vice versa. But that's not the point. You simply cannot escape your destiny, so however much is your fate is how much you drink. Not more, not less, but exactly as much. However much is in there you have to try and drink it, a little, or conversely, a lot."

"What's in the barrel?"

"What do you mean?"

"Well, is it vodka, or beer, or wine? Or maybe champagne? Or a mixture of all of them?

"Good question. You know what's in there, most likely? Pure spirit. You see, every alcoholic drink has a spirit content: four percent in beer, forty percent in vodka, seventeen percent in port. The barrel depends not on how much of which drink you drink—that would be a bit much, even Gosplan couldn't make sense of that one—but on the content of spirit in all the drinks.[26] That's the only way it could work. Don't you think?"

I nodded.

"So here's the plan. Tomorrow morning we'll head to the Institute of Lift and Transport Equipment, and then we'll have two hours left to go to the stores. We need to buy some good sausage for sure, and marshmallow-filled chocolates, and a couple boxes of those other chocolates for Natasha and Mama. They have those chocolates here. What are they called? 'Charming' or something? No, 'Inspirational', that's what they're called."

Our room was in a section with one other room, a single. Next to our two beds and the night stands was an armchair, a writing table, and an old television on a lacquered nightstand. I went over to the television and pressed the red button. It warmed up, sputtering. Grey and black stripes appeared on the screen. I turned the dial. There wasn't a single channel transmitting.

"You can go ahead and get comfortable," said Papa. "I'll go wash up, then you can. And then we'll go to bed because there's so much more to do tomorrow."

Papa left the room. There was a green telephone on the table.

We didn't have one at home. I picked up the receiver and pressed six numbers at random. There was silence in the receiver. I dialed one more number, a seven.

I heard a buzz, then another. Something clicked and the receiver connected.

"Hello!" said a woman's voice. "Hello… Is anybody there? If you don't want to say anything, I guess that's your business."

The receiver clicked again. There was a short buzz. I pressed the lever and dialed more numbers at random. A girl picked up. She might have been the same age as me.

"Hello," she said softly. "Is that you again, Tisha? How long are you going to breathe into the receiver? This is the fifth time you've called today."

I put the receiver down.

I went down to the landing between the first and second floors, unbolted our mailbox and took out the *Komsomolskaya Pravda* and the *Mogilev Pravda*.

Yakimovich was coming up the stairs from below. His jacket was unzipped, he had a big fat briefcase with him and like always, he was drunk.

"Hello."

"Hello, hello." His voice wasn't very pleasant. It was weak. He sounded like a woman. "Why haven't I seen your mama and papa around?"

"They went on vacation. To the sanatorium on Lake Naroch."

"A vacation, that's good. I'm supposed to have a voucher coming to me too. It's from the union committee at the tech institute in August. Where did that bucket disappear to?"

"What bucket?"

"Remember there used to be one of those buckets here on every landing. For the food scraps."

"They got rid of those a long time ago," I said. "Two or three years ago."

"Really? I never even noticed," he said. "I never threw my scraps in there. I couldn't see how scraps would help them start the food program. Did your mama and papa throw stuff in there?"

"I don't remember."

Three or four years before there was an iron bin with a lid on every landing with "Food Scraps" written on it and next to building #146 there was a box that had a big barrel for the scraps. On the box was a picture of a pig's face and the words: "Food Program— For Life." The scraps were supposed to get hauled away to feed pigs somewhere but they tended to get really stinky and gross.

Yakimovich started fiddling with his mailbox. I went up to our apartment, took off my slippers, tossed the newspapers on the little table in the entry, and peeked in the living room. Natasha was sitting at the table with her textbooks. Lesha was on the couch tuning his guitar.

I asked, "When are you going to teach me to play?"

"Right now. But we should go in your room so we don't bother Natashka."

We relocated to the bedroom. Out the window, the green leaves were shivering in the wind. The wind was driving the clouds across the sky above the kindergarten.

Lesha sat on my bed. He was wearing *Super Perry's* brand jeans with zippers on the back pockets and a black shirt with a small "Moscow" tag on it.

"Here, look. This chord is very easy, E Minor. Press two strings on this fret, fifth, and sixth. Try it," he said.

I put two fingers on the fret board. Lesha strummed the strings. They made a sour sound.

"Press harder. So it'll sound clean. Can you hear how it's better now? Now try again."

"Did you teach yourself to play or did somebody teach you?" I asked.

"A little of both. At first I went to a guy in my building. Wait, I take it back. Even before that my papa gave me a 'teach yourself' book. It was *Teach Yourself To Play Six String Guitar*, it's still lying around at home somewhere. But I didn't really get anything out of it. It was all about notes and that was useless to me. But I wanted to play, so then I went to this guy Rodion. He showed me the primary chords and I learned a few more by myself. Then in tenth grade the school got some instruments and we put together an ensemble."

"Where did you play?"

"A few times at school dances, then at the tire retreading factory. You might say that was the peak of our career," Lesha laughed. He took a pack of *Kosmos* and matches out of his shirt pocket, took out a cigarette, and lit up.

"What songs did you play?"

"Lots of different ones. There still wasn't any Italian music around back then. That stuff is shit. We played The Earthlings. 'Believe in Your Dreams', 'I Beg Your Pardon, Planet Earth', 'Stunt Man'. The Earthings are shit too, really, but at that point nobody was really listening to cool music. That came later at the institute.

Oh yeah, we played stuff from Time Machine: 'For Those Who Are At Sea', 'The Curve', 'Blue Bird'. That's more or less what we played from them. Dynamic is all around better, though." Lesha inhaled then tapped his ashes in the vase of violets. "Here's another chord, look, G Major. It's more complicated, you have to spread your fingers really wide, but you can try—maybe put them like... yeah, like that. Try again and it will sound right—yeah, there it is, better."

"Did you have to be good to play in the ensemble?"

"Of course not, not really—especially at the beginning. There was only one guy who could play with some skill, Kolya Yevseyenko. Now he's at the Teacher's Institute and he plays in an ensemble at the Dnieper restaurant. When he was with us he played guitar solos and sang. I was on rhythm guitar, Shmir was on bass, and Pleskachev was on drums. Isn't there an ensemble at the school anymore?"

"I haven't heard of anything like that," I said.

"Probably not, but Natashka would know for sure. I'm sure they must still have some of the instruments. We didn't wreck them in our day and they couldn't have just thrown them away. Maybe they made like they threw them away and then sold them to somebody."

Lesha opened the balcony door and flicked out his butt.

"Here, memorize the fourth chord and you can play this song."

Lesha took the guitar from me, tuned the first string, and began to sing:

Their faces are worn off, their paint is faded
I can't tell if they're people or they're dolls

They stare just like a stare, their shadows like shadows
I'm getting so tired, I have to take a rest
But I invite you to a showcase
Where the dolls look just like people.

Lesha put the guitar down on the bed.

"What's that song?" I asked.

"Wow, I'm surprised. You should be ashamed you don't know Time Machine. For some reason you have a hard time with this stuff, you and Natashka both. I want to make a tape of something for her so she won't just listen to any old shit, and you too. The number one group is Dynamic, then Time Machine. Then, well, Primus is okay. 'A girl in the bar today, fifteen year's old girl, a skinny guy beside her, they've only three rubles between them—'"

"Do you know Sergei Novoselov?" I asked him. "He lives in building #150, finished school last year. He's studying in Minsk now at RTI. He listens to metal."

"Metal is shit. Metal and Italian music—they're nothing but shit. What, you like metal?"

"Of course not, not really."

"Let's see if Natashka will make us something to eat," he said. "What is there in the refrigerator, do you know?"

I couldn't sleep because of the heat, tossing and turning in bed for over an hour. Lesha stayed with us overnight. The light in the living room had been out for a long time but they didn't turn off the music. Probably so I wouldn't hear them fucking. As if I didn't know why he stayed over. I quietly got out of bed, went to the bedroom door, and opened it a little. The couch creaked in the living room and then the carpet rustled. The door opened. Natasha came out with nothing on. I caught a glimpse of the black hair between her legs. The door of the living room stayed open. Lesha was sitting on the fold-out couch, which was folded out into its bed shape. He was leaning against the rug that hung on the wall. The light went on in the bathroom and the door creaked. Lesha took a cigarette out of his pack, struck a match, and lit up. Water started running in the bathroom.

★

Lesha and I walked up to the Worker's bus stop. A couple guys from A class—Volkovich and Yurchik—were sitting on the bench. I nodded to them. They didn't respond but looked at Lesha.

"I don't understand people who listen to foreign rock," said Lesha. "I'm gonna estimate they'll pay seventy five rubles for one record, and if it's a double album it's a full hundred. Plus, they can't understand the lyrics since none of it's in Russian. I'd rather make a tape of the new Dynamic or Time Machine, all for just a fiver. That music is totally obnoxious and you can't understand the words. The words are the most important thing to me. If I don't understand what they're singing about, there's no point in listening to it."

I nodded.

"Did you play while I was gone today?" asked Lesha. He had been leaving his guitar at our place so I could practice.

"Yeah, a little. My fingers hurt."

"And they will hurt. You know how much skin has to peel off

107

your fingers before you can start playing in earnest? But it's worth it. For yourself, and the girls like it too." Lesha made a kissing face.

The trolleybus rolled up. Lesha and I got on and went to the last platform.

"I told Natashka to have your parents buy a reel-to-reel and give you her little tape player," he said.

"They won't buy one. I heard them say we don't have the money right now."

"That's too bad. That would be a cool machine for her and you'd have a good tape player to start out with. Then later you could upgrade to a reel-to-reel."

"What kind do you have at home?" I asked.

"A *Rostov-102*, plus a Corvette amplifier and AS-50 speakers—pretty decent quality. You'll see what I mean when we get there."

We went out on Ordzhonikidze, turned on Lenin and went past Toys. I didn't want to go in there with Lesha. I didn't want him to think I was interested in that stuff, like I was still a little kid.

"Wanna go to the beer hall by The Wench later?" asked Lesha.

"By what?"

"The garment factory club," he said. "They call it The Wench Club, or just 'The Wench'. A bunch of the wenches from the garment factory hang out there. The beer is usually fresher there. You still don't drink beer, do you? Or have you started drinking by now?"

"No, I don't drink yet."

"Well it's no big deal, you'll start soon. 'All in good time.' They used to say that in Ancient Greece, you know."

We went up to the wooden recording kiosk on the corner of Lenin and Fire Station Lane. There was a list of albums nailed to the wall of the recording kiosk—written by hand:

Time Machine—'82, '83-I, '83-II, '84, '85
Dynamic—'83, '84, '85

Lesha took one of Natasha's Sony cassettes out of his pocket. Papa brought her three of them from Leningrad.

The curly red haired guy in the kiosk picked up a piece of paper and looked at us. "What you wanna tape?" he asked.

I unlocked the apartment door and knocked loudly. I did this in certain situations. The door to the living room was open a little. Music was playing, the Dynamic concert that Lesha and I taped at the recording kiosk:

When I got tired of wandering
It made me think of Moscow
And all the people's multicolored
Dreams swirling in their heads
A sun beam was smiling
It took me back home
Where everyone who loved me
Was right there waiting.

Natasha looked out from the living room, red in the face and laughing.

"Congratulate me! I got in!"

She gave me a smooch on the cheek. Lesha looked out too and gave me a nod.

"And who do you need to thank? Me and your bra. For our support in this difficult time of your life," he said.

"Thank you," Natasha told him. She gave me another smooch then suctioned onto Lesha's lips for a long time. He stroked her back under her white t-shirt.

"So let's celebrate, wash your hands, and join us," Natasha said to me.

There was a bottle of *Agdam* port on the magazine table. It was about half empty. The remnants of a clove cake sat in its box. Lesha took two cigarettes out of his pack of *Kosmos* and looked at me.

"You don't want to smoke, do you?"

"Sure, I'll smoke."

"You're allowed to today," said Natasha. "You're allowed to do anything on a day like today. And have a drink for me, too. Just a little one, it's symbolic."

She took one of the thin, delicate glasses with a pattern on it—the ones she and Mama drank from at family feasts while everybody else drank from thick glasses—and poured me half a glass.

"Here, have some."

I took the glass, had a taste, and made a face.

"You've got a lot ahead of you," said Lesha. "Mark my words. Two years from now you'll be looking for any opportunity to have a drink, and it will be more and more complicated to do so. You've probably heard about this 'war on drunkenness and alcoholism' tripe? You know how long you have to stand in line for vodka now? And now they're selling just two bottles at a time. So drink up, kid, before they dump it all out."

I drank the port in one gulp, put the glass on the table, lit up my cigarette, and inhaled. Natasha poured glasses for Lesha and herself. They clinked glasses, had a drink, and started kissing. Their cigarettes were smoking away in the ashtray. The song "Sportloto" was playing. *Kharkov Metallists are this country's number one football team!* yelled Kuzmin, the singer. The audience cheered and clapped.

"This concert was apparently in Kharkov," said Lesha.

He leaned over and picked up a piece of paper off the floor— it had fallen off the magazine table.

"That's a composition from one of Mama's pupils," said Natasha.

"Composition on the theme of my favorite toy," read Lesha. "I have a doll. Her name is Dasha. I love her, but she has crooked legs. But I'm not offended that she has crooked legs."

He chuckled. Natasha and I did too.

"Are you going to do your club again in September?" asked Natasha.

"I don't know. Maybe I will, maybe I won't."

"Well, do you want to?"

"I haven't thought about it," I said.

"That's a bunch of crap, not a club," said Lesha. "Natasha was telling me about that coach of yours. He'll be kicked out for being a drunk soon if what she said is true. In the past he could have slipped by, but there's no way now. I'm telling you, they need to do an ensemble at the school. Now that would be cool. But motorized models? That's kid's stuff."

"There are seventeen-year-old guys who go to the club."

"They can go, that's their business. But I'm talking about you," he said. Lesha opened the window, stuck his head out, and looked down. I went up beside him. Two drunk men were walking on the little street.

"The war on drunkenness hasn't done a thing," Lesha muttered. "Anybody who used to drink still drinks, only now it's not rotgut wine, it's glass cleaner and tinctures."

"Tell those stories to somebody else," Natasha laughed. "They don't really drink tinctures."

"If I say something, it means I know it," said Lesha. "I have a neighbor, Uncle Grisha, he's been hammered every day for the last ten years. And then he had to stand in line when they restricted liquor sales, then vodka prices went up, so he made the switch to tinctures. I'll introduce him to you if you want."

"Fine, I believe you. I don't need to meet him. But I can't imagine how somebody could really drink that stuff."

"I read in *Traffic Safety* magazine about a guy who ate a car," I said. "Somewhere in England or France. Every day he sawed off a piece of his Morris Mini, crushed it down really fine and swallowed it. And then they wrote, 'It's astonishing that he managed to survive for several years after that.'"

I pushed my bike out the gate, took a rag out of my bike holster, and wiped down the splash guard and frame. This summer I hadn't really added anything new to my bike, just a sticker on my bike holster of a *Lada-2106* car. I got it in Moscow.

Two guys were standing by the pump and drinking something from a little bottle with a gold sticker. Little bottles like these got thrown into Babushka's garden—her fence was right next to pump. The stickers said "Calendula Tincture".

"Hey man, you off on a world tour?" asked one.

I didn't answer. I pushed off the asphalt, threw my leg over the frame, sat down and pushed the pedals.

"Fucking stop!" yelled a guy in a yellow t-shirt and shabby sweat pants. He and two others were standing outside the store in Tishovka—the village that was just on the other side of the railroad. I was already past the store and they couldn't catch up with me. I gave them the finger.

I rode quickly on the left side of the road, against the flow of traffic like Papa taught me so I could see all the vehicles coming on my side. I passed the monument to The Unknown Soldier, the football field, and a single story wooden school. The trees ended. The road was now running parallel to the railroad. The Tishovka Cemetery and the crossroads with the railroad to Minsk were up ahead.

I stood up on the pedals so I wouldn't bump my butt as I went across the tracks. At the three-road fork I took the middle, riding on the asphalt. A hundred meters from the road there was a tall haystack. I leaned my bike against it, stood on the cargo rack, then on the seat, and climbed up on top. Visible in the distance was apartment building #170-B in Worker's, the trucking company, the wooden houses on Uspensky and Ivan Franko, and the lightning rod and the silo tower in Tishovka.[27] Our building was hidden behind the trees. I lay on my back. The sky was blue and cloudless.

★

I was riding fast so I could speed past the store as quickly as possible in case those guys were still there.

"Stop! Get him!"

I turned around. There was another guy with them now, this one on a moped. The beginning of a cornfield was on the right.

"Stop! I'm gonna nail you!" hollered the guy on the moped.

There were five hundred meters left before the turnoff to Worker's. The guy on the moped caught up with me and was riding beside me.

"Hit your brakes you little shit!" he screamed and pushed me.

I fell with my bike into the corn. The guy stopped, got off his moped, and came over to me.

"You can get outta here. The bike stays with us," he chuckled.

The rest ran up.

"How come you took off?" said a guy in a yellow shirt. Then he punched me in the gut.

"Really? The bike's no good, huh?" The other guy touched the fender with the reflectors on it.

"Where'dja get them there reflectors? Who'dja steal 'em from?"

"I bought them at Sporting Goods."

"No shit," he said.

"Anyway, take off all your reflectors and the fender then you're outta here. Got that?" The guy in the yellow shirt grabbed me by the shirt and shook me, then let me go. I unlatched my holster and

114

took out my wrench.

★

Lesha and Natasha were sitting on the couch, watching television with their arms around each other. The old comedy *Hello, I'm Your Aunt* was on, closed-captioned for some odd reason.

"How'd you get so dirty?" asked Natasha.

"Some thugs in Tishovka made off with my reflectors and the splash guard."

"I told you not to ride around there by yourself," she said.

"Lesha, let's go. Come with me and we'll go find them," I said.

Lesha glanced at the screen, then at me. "Where were they from?"

"I don't know, they were village thugs. It's not far from here, fifteen minutes on foot. Or maybe we should take my bike. You can be on the seat and I'll ride on the cargo rack or the frame."

"You know what I'm going to say about this, Igor? You need to solve problems like these by yourself. Sure, I could go with you, but what good would that do? We could go back there and assuming we get your reflectors—that is, if we can even get them back. Maybe they already sold them. And even if they didn't, I doubt they'd be just sitting there waiting for us to show up. You need to learn to stand up for yourself. If you can stand up for yourself, you can protect yourself in such a way that nobody will ever touch you."

"That's easy for you to say," Natasha interrupted him. "You took judo for five years. Of course you can stand up for yourself."

"Yes, I did, but that doesn't matter. If you're going up against strength you're head has to be in the game. Strength isn't just in

115

your hands, it's up here," he touched his forehead with his finger. "You have to find the right words to use on these thugs so they won't touch you. Got it?"

I nodded.

"And don't get so worked up over a bunch of reflectors. That stuff is bullshit, nothing but affectations."

"Go have some lunch," Natasha told me. I went in the bathroom for a minute. In the living room, I heard her say quietly, "The main reason you blew him off is that you didn't want to go with him, didn't you? Be honest, I'll understand."

"No, that's what I really think," Lesha said. "Let him learn how to stand up for himself. You think I never got my butt kicked? It happened a bunch of times."

"They started a temperance society at my school," said Mama. "There was an order from the district that every school must have a temperance society."

The three of us were sitting on the couch—Mama, Natasha, and me. The news was on the television.

"The first thing at the teacher's meeting was a discussion to pick a chairman. Seletskaya suggested the military instructor Semyon Sergeevich, but he wouldn't have anything to do with it. 'I partake,' he said."

"Is he an alcoholic?" asked Natasha.

"Well, not an alcoholic, of course. No school would keep him on if he was an alcoholic. He probably just gets drunk now and then. He's said as much."

"Who did they choose then?" I asked.

"You know all the teachers at Mama's school now?" Natasha laughed.

"No, I'm just interested."

"They chose the gym teacher, Gomonkov."

"He doesn't drink at all?" asked Natasha.

"I don't know. He might drink. He just didn't let it be known."

"So what, are they going to force all the teachers to attend?"

"We don't know yet. Just that the district ordered it."

The lock clicked. I heard a noise in the entryway. Papa looked into the living room, leaning his hand on the doorframe.

"Why are you walking in here in your boots?" asked Mama.

"It's not such big deal, don't get all worked up. You shouldn't worry so much about these things."

The yard of the neighbor Bogolyubov was visible through Babushka's kitchen window. Yulka—she was in third grade— was tossing a kitten up in the air and catching it. Bogolyubov was holding two kittens and the mother cat. There had been a third but some kids hung it from a tree by the motor factory.

Babushka offered me a fat *blin* smeared with butter and cut into four pieces. I picked up a piece and took a bite.

The apartment door shut. Uncle Zhora came in wearing old worn jeans, their leg bottoms patched with leather so they wouldn't fray, and a black corduroy jacket. He was carrying his briefcase. He set the briefcase on the floor and shook my hand.

"Well, how's everyone doing?" he asked as he pulled a chair

up to the table.

"How do you think we're doing?" asked Babushka. "You know me, from morning to evening I'm in the garden. You show up but you never help."

"I know you understand why, Mama. I told you long ago that if I'm going to spend time in the garden it can only be to the extent of my strength and interest. Covering the raised bed, digging potatoes—I'm always ready to help with that stuff. But tilling the soil, that's not my—anyway, how goes it for the younger generation?" He winked at me.

"School started," I said.

"For some reason you say this without joy."

"How could there be joy?"

"What, nothing's interesting at all? Isn't there one subject you like?"

"Nah."

"That's no good," he said. "Although it does depend on the teachers. In fact, it all depends on them."

Babushka set a plate in front of Uncle Zhora and put a *blin* on it, just like she had for me.

"I have a little something to go with the *blini*," Uncle Zhora got up, bent down to his briefcase and took out two bottles of *Zhigulevskoye* with the yellow stickers. "Want a beer?" he asked me.

"What are you doing? He's still too young for beer," said Babushka. "Especially these days, they're having a whole war so the kids won't start drinking."

"He can have a little," said Uncle Zhora. "Get us two glasses."

Babushka set the glasses on the table. Uncle Zhora opened the bottle and poured me half a glass, himself a whole one. We clinked glasses. I took a drink. I didn't really like the bitter taste of beer, but everybody else was drinking it, which had to mean there was something good about it.

"Have you heard anything about an apartment?" asked Babushka.

"There's nothing right now. You know the drill. You have to get on the list ten years in advance. Right now there won't be anything right away. That's the minimum—ten years. Especially the waiting list for our neighborhood."

"So you're going to spend the whole time in that hostel? Why won't you move in with me? The room is empty anyway, there's plenty of space."

"But you know it's great for me, I love my independence. I'll always be a little boy to you. You'll always try to control me. My every move."

"You need to get married, Zhora," said Babushka.

"No, Mama, don't even talk about it. He who gets burnt once by milk forever blows on water. It's a stupid proverb but it's true."

I was writing my chemistry assignment in one of my Moscow brand school notebooks, the kind with the nice paper. Papa and I bought ten of them over the summer in Moscow: half for me, half for Natasha. The wind was shaking the yellow leaves outside the window. Lesha and Natasha were talking in the living room behind the closed door. The bedroom door was closed too and I couldn't hear anything. I pulled up my chair, went up to the door and opened it a little.

"Well, what am I supposed to say to you?" said Lesha. "Wait for me and I'll come back, right? Two years, that's a long time, and I don't want all the usual banality: the letters, the tears, the promises. That's, well, I don't know, on par with how the peasants do it or something."

"I never had any idea you'd be going off to the army like this."

"And that's a good thing, you didn't have any preconceptions. It's better not to have any ideas about what will happen tomorrow. We should just live today for today."

"I don't want you to leave."

"As if I want to. You can thank Andropov, or whoever it was that decided to conscript students.[28] Up until now they wouldn't take us since we already had the military classes and all that."

"You're changing the subject. It doesn't matter to you. You don't care if you're leaving or not because you don't give a damn about me."

"That's not true and you know it. But I don't want us to be tied to each other or something for two whole years, you know? That's stupid."

"You bastard!" screamed Natasha. "You don't give a shit about me! You're a fool! Get out! Go fuck yourself!"

I'd never heard Natasha use profanity like that. I shut the bedroom door. The living room door opened sharply. Lesha came out and went to the entryway.

Kolya and I went around the pharmacy and crossed the street. The letters on building #150 were already lit up: *Slava KPSS,*

"Praise the Communist Party of the Soviet Union!" Two years ago the "L" fell off. It was lucky nobody got killed. They put a new one up this year on May Day. In the daytime you could tell something was different about the new "L" but at night when they were lit up all the letters looked the same.

A sweet smell was coming from the deli. They were probably baking pirozhki.[29] The two-story building next to the cafeteria was cordoned off with a wood fence for repairs.

"Did I tell you my babushka used to live in that house?" I asked. "Up until the war."

"That really old house?" asked Kolya.

"Yeah. It was built in 1937 or '38. When my grandfather came back from the war they moved into the house on Motor Street. And you know who later lived in that very same house where Babushka used to live?"

"No. How would I know?"

"Melenkov, he was in our class until fourth grade. Remember?"

"Of course I remember. We were in the same kindergarten too. #51."

"Did you ever go to his house?"

"No."

"I did one time. It was one huge room and it had a stove in it that took up the whole corner. And no hot water, only cold, and the toilet was outside. Then his parents got an apartment in Schmidt and they moved."

In the vacant lot between the trucking company and building #170-B some guys were playing football. It was dark but the flood-light from the trucking company lit up the field.

"Let's go over there, you want to watch them play?" I asked.

"Eh, I don't feel like it."

"Alright," I said. We crossed the street.

"Are you going to do your club again this year?" asked Kolya.

"No."

"Why?"

"I don't want to. I don't feel like it. They can kiss my ass," I said.

"You could win another *Smena*."

"What would I do with it? Pickle it? I already have two. I can give you one."

"I don't need one. I don't care about taking pictures," he said.

"Let's join the biking club, what do you say?" I asked him.

"Which one?"

"I don't know, wherever they have one—maybe at the Pioneer Palace or the stadium."

"You like racing bikes?"

"Well, sure. Don't you?"

"Not really. You look like a fool sitting on a racing bike with your butt up in the air," he said.

"Like hell I look like a fool," I said.

"No, I don't want to. I don't have time. I'm working on my receiver."

"What kind?"

"It's a standard radio receiver."

"What will you be able to listen to on it?"

"You mean, which waves?"

"Yeah."

"Different ones. Longwave, shortwave."

There were two trolleybuses by the Green Meadows stop. We walked past the repair pit. There was standing water in it with patches of oil at the bottom. We crossed paths with Oksana from Kolya's building—who was walking down the road holding hands with some guy.

"Why didn't you say hi to her?" I asked.

"I never say hi to her. When I was little she always laughed at me and made fun of me."

"What about now?"

"She stopped that stuff a long time ago."

"How old is she?" I asked.

"I don't know. Nineteen or twenty," he said. "She's a third year at the engineering institute. You saw who she was fucking. He was at least thirty-five."

"How do you know they're fucking? May they're just going for a walk. Or they're getting married."

"An older guy wouldn't just go for a walk like that. They're fucking. Totally. Does your sister fuck her guy? What's his name? Lesha, right?"

"How would I know? That's none of my business."

"I didn't say it was your business. I'm just asking."

"And I answered that I don't know. That's all. End of discussion."

"Whatever," he said. "Maybe we should go home."

"Alright, let's go," I said. We turned around and went back. There wasn't anybody in the yellow vehicle inspection booth today. The window was shuttered. There was usually an inspector standing there with a stick stopping cars.

A strange smell was coming from the kitchen, like gas. I yanked my feet out of my shoes without untying the laces and hung up my jacket. The living room door opened and Papa came out.

"Why are you home?" I asked him.

"I took the day off," he said. "I needed to go somewhere."

"Why does it stink like gas?"

"Natasha forgot to turn it off. It was an accident."

"Where is she?"

"She's here. Don't worry. Everything's fine. Have something to eat."

"I don't want anything right now," I said.

I took the *Model Enthusiast* magazine I had out of my briefcase. Guron gave it to me. He thought maybe I'd buy it off him, but I wasn't planning on buying it, just looking at it. I sat at the table with the magazine. The door opened and shut. Mama's boots clicked across the floor. The living room door hinges creaked.

"What happened?" yelled Mama. "Care to explain it to me?"

"Quiet!" said Papa. "Igor's home. Go close the door."

I got up, went to the bedroom door and opened it a little.

"Well, thankfully everything turned out okay. I'd say it was lucky I came home from work when I did. Can you even imagine what might have been? It's a good thing she'd only just turned the gas on."

"Where was your head?" Mama hollered at Natasha. "We left you alone for three weeks thinking you could behave yourselves. But you took it as an opportunity to crawl into bed with a boy."

"That's none of your business. I'm a grown woman," said Natasha.

"Would you listen to that? A grown woman! You're going to drive me to an early grave with your escapades! A grown woman."

"Alright, let's discuss this calmly," said Papa. "We need to do something here, make a decision."

"Why is it you think you should be a part of any decision making?" Mama screamed. "You've never given a damn about anything, you never parent her at all!"

"Oh, and you parent her?"

"When would I have the time? All day long I'm at school, and then I grade notebooks until late at night. If I had the time—"

"And if I had the time."

"Shut up!" Mama yelled. "I've heard quite enough out of you already."

I went back to the table. The magazine was open to a page with the schematic of a Messerschmitt airplane on it.

Natasha walked across the room, took something out of the entertainment center, and threw it in her old 1980 Olympics bag. I sat on the couch and watched her. The tape deck was playing at a low volume:

Someday all the pain will die, and the wise man says:
Every bonfire burns down eventually,
The ashes will scatter in the wind without a trace.

"I'll come see you in the hospital," I said.

"You don't have to. Alright? There's no need. It's just for a few days."

"Okay," I said. "Did Lesha already leave for the army?"

Natasha didn't answer, just left the room. I went over to the television, picked up the *Youth Banner* newspaper, and looked at the schedule. Nothing good was marked for today.

Natasha came back with her toothbrush and a tube of mint toothpaste.

Makarevich sang:

The one who burned all the wood
In just an hour was wrong
And once that hour was over
The big fire burned right down,
But in that one hour
Everybody felt warm.

I went up to the window. There was a wedding procession going down the street—a gray *Volga* and two *Lada-6* cars, blue and red. All the cars were decorated with ribbons. A doll was attached to the hood of the *Volga*.

Colorful pin-ups of various foreign rock groups from the German magazine *Melodie und Rhytmus* hung on the walls of my uncle's room. A teakettle was boiling on the hotplate. The Toshiba tape deck was playing some non-Russian rock. Uncle Zhora bought the tape deck at the consignment shop when he got back from his expedition at the end of the summer.

"Uncle Zhora," I began. "As far as what happened between Natasha and Lesha—"

"I can't tell you very much about that. In my opinion, what happened was caused by their moral infantilism. Do you know this word?"

"No."

"Well, you might call it 'underdevelopment,' but underdevelopment, that sounds too harsh. I wouldn't want to insult them because they're good kids. I do like Lesha. Of course, I only met him the one time. You have to understand, the main problem with that age is that when you say something to them, really try to explain something, it's pointless." Uncle Zhora got up from the table, picked up the kettle, and poured the boiling water in the teapot on the table. There were two drinking bowls beside it. He brought them back from Uzbekistan and only ever drank his tea from one of them, never from a teacup.

"You still listen to me for now. But they're already to the point where they don't listen. They learn everything by trial and error. And an error sometimes brings some very expensive tears. But by then there's nothing they can do about it."

The tape deck clicked—the cassette was over. The auto-reverse turned on and the tape switched to the other side.

"Here's the main thing I can say about all this," said Uncle Zhora. "Life goes on. That's what I told Natasha."

"Do you think he'll come back to her?" I asked.

"Lesha? That's unlikely. Two years is too long. Besides that, you can't step twice in the same river. He'll come back a different man from the one who left. The army changes people every time. I have to say—I don't think it's necessary for them to wait for each

127

other for two years, like it's somehow a testament to their feelings and what have you. That's all nonsense."

"Did you tell her all that?"

"Not in so many words. But of course she had no interest in listening."

Mama and I were sitting on the couch, Natasha in the armchair. The WWII movie *Fiery Roads* was on the television. The light in the living room was dim—one of the bulbs in the chandelier had burnt out a long time ago. Papa forgot to change it, and I had been lazy about it too.

The front door clicked and opened. Papa came in, shut the door and turned the lock. He made a lot of noise as he pulled off his jacket and took off his boots. Natasha kept looking at the screen and wouldn't look away. Papa came up and stood in the doorway, holding on to the doorframe.

"You're loaded again?" asked Mama. "What were you celebrating today? You're going to find yourself in a mess one of these days. They'll pick you up on the trolleybus and take you away to sober up, and then they'll send a letter to the factory about you. Especially now that they're getting so strict about it."

"Quiet! Some of us are trying to watch the movie!" yelled Natasha.

Papa went in the bedroom and closed the door behind him.

"You didn't need to be so obnoxious," Mama turned to Natasha. "There wasn't anything so important about that movie."

"It's just disgusting for me to have to listen to that. Go in the other room if you've got a score to settle with him."

"It's not your place to tell me what to do."

"Alright, everybody calm down," I said.

"And you can just sit there and be quiet when nobody's talking to you," Mama said to me.

Papa's snore was audible from the bedroom.

A bunch of guys were crowded around Kuzmenok's desk. I went over and got in between Strelchenko and Kravtsov. Kuzmenok had some playing cards with naked babes on them spread out on the desk—they weren't the real cards, they were photocopies of the originals.

"Who'd you buy these from, Gypsy Boy?" asked Kravtsov.

"None of your business who I bought them from," Kuzmenok said. "This one's not bad, huh?"

There was a babe with long hair on the card photographed from behind. She was on her knees.

"This one's pretty fucking good," said Kravtsov. "You can see the pussy really well. I'd stick it in her."

Kuzmenok looked at him. "What do you mean, stick it in her?"

"What do I mean? You don't get it?"

"No, but I'm sure you'll tell me," Kuzmenok said. "I'm pretty dense, huh?"

"What your problem?" said Kravtsov.

"What's my problem? Like you know anything about that stuff? Do you know what jizz is? Do you know how to fuck? Have you seen fucking somewhere? No? So what the hell do you think you're talking about with this 'stick it in her'?

"Like you've ever seen anybody do it," said Kravtsov. "Or maybe you've done some fucking yourself, huh? Nah, you've only ever seen the way your mama fucks. Everybody knows how much she likes entertaining the men."

Kuzmenok socked Kravtsov in the jaw. Kravtsov flew off the desk, landed on his butt in the aisle, and banged his head on the table. He got up and left the classroom. The bell rang. Kuzmenok shoved the cards in his briefcase.

Five minutes went by in history. The history teacher was leafing through a magazine and picking her ear with the earpiece of her glasses. The door of the classroom opened and the vice principal came in.

"Excuse me, Ludmilla Nikolaevna. You might say we have a crisis on our hands," she said, and closed the door. "Kids, I have a very serious question for you. It has come to my attention that one of you has some cards with indecent subject matter on them. Very indecent subject matter, I must say. I think you all understand that it is prohibited for you to look at such cards, and that it's prohibited even more so to bring them with you to school. We will of course endeavor to gain an understanding of how they showed up and where they came from, but right now it is far more important to me that the one who brought them to school today confesses himself. Honestly and candidly like a good Pioneer. This does not mean that he will be immediately excused because this infraction is really quite serious, but with a confession we can strike a plea bargain, as you know from detective films. So, which of you brought these indecent cards to school?"

Kolya turned to me and whispered, "What do you think, who snitched on him? Kravtsov?"

"Hardly," I said. "Kuzmenok would totally kill him if he did." The back of Kravtsov's head had bandages stuck all over it. There was dried blood in his hair below the bandages.

"But who then?"

"I don't know. There are plenty of snitches in this class," I said.

"Kids," said the vice principal. "I don't mean to alarm you, but if the guilty person doesn't confess by himself, it may be the case that everyone will have to be punished. I'll wait exactly one more minute."

Kuzmenok stood up.

"Come with me," said the vice principal. "And bring your bag."

Kuzmenok walked down the aisle shuffling his slippers. The vice principal opened the door. Kuzmenok went out, the vice principal behind him.

"What will happen to him?" asked Nevedomtseva. "He'll get kicked out of school, right?"

The history teacher put her glasses on. "They won't kick him out of school, but they will be having a very serious conversation. How could he have sunk to this level?"

The lights came on in the theater. The credits were rolling on the screen. People were pouring out of the movie hall. There was a big crowd even though the movie was shit—*The Battle of Moscow.*

I'd seen like a hundred thousand different films about the war but only a few were any good, maybe only *Seventeen Moments of Spring.*[30]

I'd already done my homework so I didn't need to hurry anywhere. I turned outside the Motherland onto Lenin. Opposite me on the other side, Papa was walking with some lady in a long black coat. She took his arm and said something. They didn't see me. I stopped, waited, then walked behind them. They turned into the courtyard of School #3, walked through it, and went out on Pioneer. Something went bang. I jumped. A kid about ten years old was standing on the steps of a three-story apartment building holding a popgun in one hand, the string from it in the other. Confetti was scattered over the trampled snow.

"Did I fucking scare you?" asked the kid.

"I'm gonna fucking scare you!" I said. The kid ran away.

Papa and the lady crossed Pioneer across from the Life Technology store, then turned in the lane next to Fruits and Vegetables and went in the entry of a five-story apartment building. A sign hung above the door: *Our building has achieved the following ranking: Model of Culture and Order.* The courtyard was narrow, behind it was the start of some single-story country houses. There was a gazebo in the courtyard, and across from it a swing with a busted chain. I went in the gazebo and sat on the bench. A guy in a black jacket, bell bottoms and big mittens came out of the building's entry, maybe a year or two older than me. He looked at me.

"You got a smoke?" I asked.

"No. Do you?" he said.

"Why would I ask you for one?"

"Fuck knows." The guy turned the corner.

It was a very cold two or three degrees, my feet were frozen in my boots. I stood up and started to walk around outside the gazebo. That didn't help. The entry door opened. Papa came out. I got down and hid behind one side of the gazebo. He was alone.

I waited until he turned the corner and then ran around the building on the other side, so I'd make it to the bus stop before him. I glanced at my watch, an old *Vostok* Papa gave me. It was quarter to ten.

I sat in the kitchen, chowing down on bread and sausage. The day before they had given Papa a pack of shortage food at the factory and it had some really good *doctorskaya* sausage in it.[31] Natasha and Mama were sitting in the living room. The front door clicked and Papa came in. He took off his boots and jacket and peeked in the living room.

"Hi," he said.

"Hi," answered Mama. "Where did you go so late?"

"It was Nikanorov's birthday. We're not allowed to have parties at work right now, so we went to his place."

"You seem too sober for a birthday."

"Well, there's the anti-booze decree and all," Papa said. He came into kitchen. "Hi, how are you?" he asked me.

"Fine," I said.

Mama and Papa had already gone to bed. I quietly closed the living room door. Natasha was sitting in the armchair reading *Youth Culture* magazine. I went in and sat on a chair.

"I saw Papa today with some lady," I said. "Then he went in her building."

"Kind of tall, with a black coat?" Natasha put her magazine down on the end table.

"Yeah."

"I saw him with her too."

"Is he leaving us?" I asked.

"No," she said.

"How do you know?"

"He's been with her a long time. She's married."

"When did you find out?" I said.

"About a year ago."

"Why didn't you tell me?"

"Are you kidding? You think I should have told you about it?" Natasha said. "You figured it out for yourself and that's just fine. Just don't get it in your head to ask him about it. Or Mama."

"Does Mama know?" I asked.

Natasha picked up her magazine and turned the page.

Mama was sitting on the couch with her *Working Woman* magazine. I was beside her and Natasha was in the armchair, her legs hugged up to her chin. The made-for-TV movie *Adventures of Elektronik* was on the television.[32]

Papa was taking the pieces of an artificial New Year's tree out of its box. He bought it two months before in *GUM* and put it right in the storage closet, since nobody had felt like trying to put it together yet. Papa put the metal pole in its three-legged stand.

Then you had to stick its "branches" on the pole.

The pole was crooked. He twisted it in different directions. It didn't help. Mama looked at it, her brow furrowed.

"That thing is supposed to be our New Year's tree?"

"Maybe it will look better with the branches," answered Papa.

"With the branches, without the branches, it doesn't matter. Crooked is crooked. Which factory is churning out such freaks of nature?"

"The Brest Factory of Plastic Products."

"Why didn't you look to see if it was crooked when you bought it?"

"Why didn't you look yourself? Two heads are better than one, you know," Papa said.

"Especially when one head has a shortage of brain cells," said Mama.

"Calm down," said Natasha. "Wouldn't it be nice if we didn't have a fight on New Year's?"

"Should I keep putting it together or not?" asked Papa. "Maybe we can go without a tree. The children are more or less grown up. What do we need a tree for?"

"No, let's put it together," begged Natasha. "Let it be how it is. What would New Year's be without a tree? And Mama, you don't need to get all bent out of shape because it's crooked. Who gives a damn? The important thing is that it's a tree."

"I don't really like having an artificial one," I said. "I wish it was real. A real one smells like a tree and this one smells like plastic."

A man was going up the stairs. He had a bottle of champagne in one hand and a box with a cake in it in the other. I recognized him. He was the one who had been walking with Oksana from Kolya's building by the Green Meadows stop.

I went out the front door of the building. A guy who wasn't very tall was carrying a Sonata tape deck. Another was carrying a big black bag. The sky was black, full of stars.

Kolya opened the door. He was in Sergei's old jeans and a blue flannel shirt. His jeans were way too big so he had them cinched with a belt. The jean material was all bunched up below the belt. I took off my jacket, which left me in my new pullover: deep blue, with a gray checkered pattern on the front. Mama had bought it at *GUM* not long before.

There was a table covered with a tablecloth in the entry room. Kolya's folks were sitting on chairs, his aunt and uncle and their daughter Svetka on the couch. They lived in the Schmidt neighborhood. Svetka was in ninth grade at School #14. I'd seen her twice before. Today she was in a green dress—her hair teased and sprayed.

Kolya unlatched the bolt and opened the window. Svetka pulled out a pack of *Kosmos* and took out a cigarette then handed the pack to Kolya and me. Each of us took a cigarette.

"Won't they smell the smoke?" I nodded toward the curtain between Kolya's room and the living room.

Kolya shook his head. "Nah. They'll be smoking themselves, right at the table."

Svetka sat on the window sill. Her knees, covered with black tights, were visible from under her dress. She inhaled and blew the smoke out the window.

I pushed aside the soldering iron and a box with a bunch of

136

radio shit in it then sat at the desk. Kolya stayed on the bed. He was picking his nose. The champagne might have made him tipsy. He, Svetka, and I had the same amount of wine to drink, but maybe he couldn't handle very much.

"You're not getting together with your class for New Year's?" I asked Svetka.

"My class isn't doing anything, but there is a party I could go to." She inhaled, trying to do a smoke ring. It wouldn't form right. "I was invited."

"Why aren't you going?"

"My folks wouldn't let me. They dragged me over here with them. At least it's better coming here than staying home."

"Why wouldn't they let you go?"

"It's a long story." Svetka inhaled, then flicked her butt out the window. I could see her cleavage down the front of her dress.

Svetka sat on the bed and straightened her dress over her knees. The fabric of her dress rubbed against her tights, making a rustle. I used to hate this sound—it was like book covers rubbing together. Now I kind of liked it.

I took out a cigarette and looked out the window. Two guys were walking on the little road that went past the building. I'd seen them around. One had a popper in his hand. He took aim—like, at me—and pulled the thread. It popped. Confetti fell onto the snow.

"Happy New Year, kid!" screamed the guy.

I turned away.

"Close the window, it's cold," said Svetka.

I got up and shut the latch with a snap. Kolya startled awake, opening his eyes. He had already managed to pass out.

"What do you think, is there any champagne left?" asked

Svetka.

Kolya shook his head.

"How do you know?" she said.

"I looked. The second bottle was already empty when we came in here."

"That's no good. There's nothing to do."

"Let's tell jokes," I suggested.

"No, jokes suck. The last think I want to do is tell jokes. I'd rather talk about something interesting," said Svetka

"Well, I don't know what to talk about," I said.

"Let's play cards," said Kolya.

"Strip cards," I added.

"Are you serious?" Svetka looked at me, then Kolya.

"Well, yeah," I said. "What, are you shy?"

"Of course not, what do I have to be shy about? It's just that it won't be a fair game, you have everything on: shirt, jeans, t-shirts, pullover, you even have a belt to take off," she nodded at Kolya. "But I just have a dress on—well, and tights."

"I'm guessing you have something else on besides that," I said.

"Of course I do. But are we really going to strip down to our underwear?"

I shrugged.

"How about next time we play strip cards," said Svetka. "This time let's just play."

A raggedy New Year's tree still in its stand was lying in the garden in front of our building. Somebody must have thrown

it out the window. Papa had already taken ours down, put it back in its box and into storage. Mama wanted to throw it away but he insisted, promised he would fix it next year.

I took off my mitten and touched the snow. It was sticky. I formed a snowball and threw it at the door of the fourth entry. It broke apart. There was a white splotch left on the door.

I went up the stairs and rang the buzzer. Kolya opened the door himself.

"You alone?" I asked. He nodded. I took off my boots and jacket and went in his room. Radio parts were spread across the table. His soldering iron was smoking.

"Isn't it boring just sitting here and soldering all the time?" I asked. "You don't even have any music on."

"Nah, it's not boring. And sometimes I put on some music, records on the Radiola."

"You got any good records?"

"Not really, I just want something on in the background. Celentano, for example."

"You listen to Celentano? That moron?"

"Sometimes."

"Didn't Sergei give you back his tape deck?" I asked. "He said he wanted to get himself a reel-to-reel."

"That won't be until the fall after his construction brigade is over. By then I'll have already built my own," said Kolya. "I just need to buy a do-it-yourself tape drive mechanism. They don't have any right now."

"Do you know if Svetka is going together with somebody right now?" I asked.

"What, do you want to go with her or something?"

"Of course not, just wondering."

"She was going with one guy from tenth but he dumped her. Or she dumped him. I don't know for sure. But you don't have a chance with her. She won't even go out with guys her own age and you're two years younger than her. You're just too young for her."

"I told you, I'm not gonna ask her out or anything, I was just asking. You want to walk around with me?"

"Nah, I don't feel like walking around today," he said. "I'd rather just stay here and solder."

"Okay. I'm going for a walk around Worker's," I said.

Kuzmenok was sitting under the bus stop shelter. He noticed me and waved. I walked over to him. He took off his mitten and stuck out his hand. I shook it.

"You got any cash?" asked Kuzmenok.

"No."

"That's too bad. If you did we could get some beer."

"At the beer hall?"

"What are you, a moron? At a store not the beer hall, they wouldn't sell it to us at the beer hall."

"They would at the store?"

"At the store we can say it's for our folks."

"And they'll believe us?"

"I buy it like that all the time."

"Alright, I gotta go," I said.

"See you," he said.

Three guys from eighth were standing outside the door of the store, shaking kids down for their kopecks. I went past the post office and the police substation. A couple of girls from A class were crossing the street opposite building #170A. They had so much make-up on that they looked like clowns.

★

In the middle row, next to Zavyalova, there was a new girl—short with short dark hair. She had a notebook in front of her with a red cover and non-Russian writing on it and a transparent ball-point pen.

"She's from Germany," Kolya whispered to me. "She'll be in our class for two months. While her papa is here on leave. He's military, stationed there."

"How do you know?"

"She told me herself. She just showed up and told me her life story. Her name is Sveta. Sveta Solovyova."

I looked at her again. She had on a regular school dress just like all the girls wore and a black apron, not a lace one or anything. Only her notebook and pen were different.

Solovyova opened her notebook to the last page, where she had a color photograph cut out of a magazine. I stood up behind my desk and looked. There were two guys in the photograph—one with dark hair, the other with light hair. They both had long hair but the darker-haired guy's was longer. It said "Modern Talking" in English underneath it.[33] Kuzmenok got up from our desk and went over to her.

"That's your boyfriend, huh?" he asked, pointing at the one

141

with dark hair.

"No, of course not. That's Thomas Anders from Modern Talking. They're a very popular group right now. You've never heard of them?"

The bell rang. Kuzmenok came back to our desk. Solovyova closed her notebook. The math teacher walked into the classroom.

There was funeral music playing in the courtyard. I ran to the entryway, threw on my jacket, and went out on the balcony. There was a *GAZ-53* truck with the sides of its bed open parked by the building's entry. The bed of the truck was covered with an old red rug. A closed, gray coffin was sitting on the rug. Two Christmas trees were attached to it. I realized that they were burying Sanya Manenok from the fifth floor. He'd been killed not long ago in Afghanistan.

Several guys from the brass section of the orchestra were standing on the concrete slab—the workmen just left it there after the heating main pipe repairs—playing their instruments. Lots of people from our building and neighboring buildings were crowded around, old and young alike. They were always sticking their noses into everything.

Manenok's mama was wailing—trying to climb on the truck. Some lady was helping her. His mama got down on her knees, draped herself over the coffin and kept wailing.

I bent down and gathered some dirty snow from the balcony floor. This was the second day of the thaw. I formed a snowball and threw it up so it would hit the fourth floor balcony. It didn't work. The snowball fell to the ground.

Manenok used to go to School #28. He was a short guy with black hair. He rode an old fold-up bike with a blue frame all the way up until tenth grade. Sometimes I saw him leave school with Ludka from the building's fourth entry. They were probably in the same class. One time they were sitting on the bench below our entry, and she opened her bag and took out a magazine. They sat there and flipped through it, then he said something to her and she punched him in the stomach—not hard, just as a joke—then again and again. He didn't defend himself, just sat there and giggled. Then Ludka got up and left.

Fifteen minutes of the class had gone by, and the zoology teacher still wasn't there. I went over to Kolya.

"Maybe we should go for a walk, what do you think? Or we could go to my house?"

"That's too much trouble," he said. "And I still need to study for geography. The teacher hasn't called on me in a long time."

"Yeah well, to hell with studying for geography. You can just say whatever when he calls on you."

"No, I'd better study."

"Suit yourself," I said. "Can you take my briefcase if I don't come back by the bell? Okay?"

"Alright," he said.

The biology classroom was on the first floor, across from the stairs to the buffet and the dining hall. Further down the hall there were the doors to the secretary's office, the Pioneer leader's office, and the principal's office, but opposite was the cloakroom and the exit.

A custodian in a shabby dress was washing the floor—pushing a mop with a wet rag on it across the tiles. There was garbage floating in her water bucket. I went outside. Kuzmenok was standing on the porch—he pretty much never went to zoology.

"Got any cigarettes?" he asked.

"None," I said.

"Let's go to the gym. Maybe there's not a class in there—we can get a ball and play."

"Okay," I said. "Let's go."

Kuzmenok pulled on the door of the gym. It was locked. He bent over and looked in the keyhole.

"Fucking looks like nobody's in there."

"Maybe they went skiing?" I suggested.

"But why would they lock the gym?"

I shrugged. A noise came from the women's locker room. Kuzmenok opened the door and looked in. Voronkova and Shaturo from eighth B were sitting on the bench. The locker room was narrow and they had their feet up on the wall. Their dresses were riding up but I couldn't see their underwear, just their thighs in their black tights. They both quickly put their legs down to the floor.

"Well, come on in since you're in here anyway," said Shaturo.

They both laughed. Kuzmenok went in.

"Do you need a special invitation or something?" Shaturo asked me. "Or are you too shy to come in the women's locker room?"

"Don't be shy, there's nothing to see here. Just a bunch of book bags," Voronkova laughed. "Nobody dressed out when they went skiing."

I went in.

"The door?" said Shaturo.

I closed the door and sat on the bench next to Kuzmenok.

"Why didn't you go skiing?" he asked.

"We couldn't go," answered Shaturo.

"Why couldn't you go?" I asked.

They both laughed.

"You guys are still kids," Boronkova laughed again. "When you grow up you'll understand."

"Hey, you shouldn't fuck with me," said Kuzmenok. "I might not take it very well." He raised his fist at Shaturo in jest.

"I might not take it very well either," Shaturo shook her fist in Kuzmenok's face.

"Who do you have for physics, the principal or Minin?" asked Voronkova.

"Minin," answered Kuzmenok. "He's a worthless piece of shit."

"We have him, too," said Voronkova. "Did you know he got a divorce and married Pavlovskaya, the math teacher? You didn't know? Yeah, well, you've always been pretty dense. The whole school is talking about it. His wife came in and got in a fight with Pavlovskaya, they were pulling each other's hair and everything."

"You saw them?" asked Kuzmenok.

"I didn't see them but people told me about it. It happened right in the middle of class. Class 5-B was there for it, that's my little sister's class. Seriously, she just ran in the room and started the fight."

"Wow," said Kuzmenok. "Then what happened?"

"Nothing. They pulled each other's hair for a while and then let each other go, and then she went and complained to the district. Minin should be kicked of the party."

"What about work, too?" asked Kuzmenok. "He's such a faggot, fuck him. They should kick him out of the school too. He's such a fucking pain in the ass. Anyway, do you have any smokes?"

"What are you gonna give us if we do?" asked Voronkova.

"What do you want?"

"Well, there's a lot of stuff we want. You tell us exactly what you have to offer."

"How about a shortbread from the buffet?"

"Don't you mean two shortbreads? One for each of us," Voronkova pouted.

"Alright, it's a deal. Two shortbreads for seven kopecks each. What kind of cigarettes do you have?"

"*Kosmos*. You didn't really think we'd have the shitty ones, did you?"

"Alright, let's go outside," said Kuzmenok.

Kuzmenok turned and exhaled, then asked the girls, "Aren't you cold? I could give you my jacket."

"That's alright, I'll manage," said Voronkova. "Otherwise you'd catch a cold or something and it would be all my fault."

Kuzmenok gave me his cigarette to hold, undid his jacket, took it off, and gave it to Voronkova. I took mine off and gave it to Shaturo.

146

"What gentlemen we have here. I had no idea," she said.

An ambulance went down Gorky Street. An old woman in a quilted jacket was leaving the bus stop with her net bag. There was a red and blue carton of milk and a round loaf of black bread in the bag.

I was going to school on a Sunday and it didn't feel normal. There were hardly any people on the street—just some school kids but even then fewer than usual. On Friday our head teacher told us that we would be studying on Sundays until the end of February, and our week would end on Thursday. They were doing this in order to economize on electricity. How this would be economical she didn't explain. Maybe she didn't understand it herself.

The day before all the guys in my class had made plans to show up without our Pioneer scarves—in our usual uniforms but with real ties and Senior Pioneer pins, which you don't get until Komsomol. We were all sick of wearing the Pioneer scarves. I rummaged around in Papa's ties for a long time. He had ten of them but they were all shitty. They were really old—ten or twenty years old, or maybe more—and one was totally ancient. It was bright blue with three swallows on a wire on it. I picked a very simple one: blue with black stripes.

The teacher looked at us.

"What on earth is this spectacle you've assembled? Have you suddenly forgotten the school uniform?"

"What's the problem?" said Kravtsov. "We're Senior Pioneers.

Why aren't we allowed to wear normal ties like regular people?"

"First of all, you'll find that Senior Pioneers are still expected to wear the Pioneer scarves. Secondly, the rules are for everyone. Pioneers must wear the red scarves. For sixty years all the Pioneers have worn them. I wore one before the war, even. Basically children, if you want to be treated like adults, you must act like adults. Tomorrow you'd best show up with your usual scarves. If you don't, our conversation will be serious. Very serious."

It had been fifteen minutes since the bell rang for geography.

"Did anybody see the geography teacher?" asked Nikolaev.

Nobody answered.

"Maybe he's just not here? Let's go for a walk."

"No, it's better if we go to somebody's apartment. Who lives nearby?" Kuzmenok said and looked at me. "Is there anybody at your place?" I nodded. "And yours?" Kuzmenok turned to Kolya.

"Nobody," said Kolya.

"What if we go over there and just hang out? We can watch *Morning Mail*."

"*Morning Mail* is on at eleven," I said.

"So what? We'll watch whatever's on when we get there." Kuzmenok slung his bag over his shoulder and walked over to the door. "Let's get out of here but not all at once, one by one. We'll meet up at the crosswalk.

"What if he shows up?" asked Zenkovich.

"He who?"

"The geography teacher."

"He won't come, don't piss yourself. But stay here if you want," said Kuzmenok. We crowded around the blackboard between the desks, the table, and the door. Only Solovyova stayed at her desk.

"You're not coming with us?" Nikolaev asked her. She shook her head.

"It isn't good to break away from the collective, you know," said Kovalenko. Solovyova turned her head and looked out the window.

"Alright, let's get going. Like we discussed," said Kuzmenok, and left.

I looked out the door. The hall was empty and the door to the teacher's lounge was closed.

Kuzmenok handed me his pack of *Astras*. I took a cigarette. He took out his matchbox and struck a match. It wouldn't light. He took out another one and lit up both of our cigarettes. We sat on the couch with Zenkovich and Zavyalova beside us.

"Want one?" Kuzmenok asked them. The girls shook their heads and turned back to the television. The show *I Serve the Soviet Union* was on.

"If the geography teacher shows up, I wonder if he'll teach class to just Solovyova." I said.

"Why do you even care? He can do whatever he wants with her, stick his dick in her even," said Kuzmenok. Zenkovich and Zavyavlova giggled.

"She thinks she's hot shit because she wears a German bra and panties," Kuzmenok kept going.

"How do you know what kind of bra she has?" asked Zenkovich. "You saw it or something?"

"I don't want to see any part of a skank like that. She can fuck herself all the way back to Germany for all I care. All the Fritzes can look at her there. I hope that bitch dies before she gets her first fuck!"

I stood up and looked in Kolya's room. Kolya, Strelchenko, and Nikolaev were playing Thousand in there. I went back in the living room and stepped out on the balcony. Mama was walking between the buildings down below. Her school was in the Leninsky District, and they weren't doing class on Sundays. I sat down so she wouldn't notice me.

Kuzmenok was sitting in the kitchen with Lenka Korsunova. They were smoking. The cigarettes had filters so they weren't Kuzmenok's *Astras*. I went over to the sink, turned on the faucet, and filled a cup with water.

Kuzmenok put his arm around Lenka. She shrugged it off.

"Why be like that? I mean, I didn't do anything," he said.

I drank my water and put the cup on the table. There was a big green kettle on the stove, just like the one we had. The refrigerator was the same as ours, too.

Kuzmenok put his arm around Lenka again. She tried to stand up but he wouldn't let go. I left the kitchen.

Morning Mail still hadn't started. There were tanks on the screen.

"'We must focus a great deal of attention on the acceleration of scientific and technological progress,' said Comrade Gorbachev, General Secretary for the Central Committee of the Soviet Union's Communist Party, in his speech during the opening of the twenty-fifth Congress," Solovyova read from a *Pravda* newspaper.

"Very good, Solovyova, excellent," said the teacher. "It appears you were quite conscientious in your preparations for *polit-info* today. And you, children, what do you have to say for yourselves?" she looked at me and Kuzmenok. "And why are you sitting together like this? Did I really seat you two together?"

I looked at my desk. Somebody had scribbled on it with a ballpoint pen then smudged it so it was impossible to read. Kuzmenok turned toward the window.

"I simply cannot understand what you two have in common," continued the teacher. "You, Razov, need to think more about your studies. Nothing you've done this quarter has been exemplary, and if you've fallen under the influence of Kuzmenok, you're going to find your grade sliding down into the three range. Alright, we're not going to waste any more time on you. If you come unprepared one more time I'll give you a zero for conduct, is that clear? Who else has something to tell us about?"

Nikolaev walked up to the front of the room staring at his newspaper and started muttering, almost to himself.

"Recently students all over the world have been observing with interest Halley's Comet in its close proximity to the Earth."[34]

Kuzmenok opened his geometry notebook and started drawing a naked babe on the last page. It didn't come out looking like anybody.

Kuzmenok tapped Korsunova on the back. She turned around. He turned the notebook toward her.

"Look, that's you" he said.

"What, you saw me? Or somebody else did? You didn't see anybody, you got that? So you know where you can stick this?" Korsunova turned back around.

"You and I will have to have a conversation about this some other time," said Kuzmenok.

"What are you gonna do to me, huh? You don't scare me you know," she said.

"You be quiet there!" yelled the teacher. "It's bad enough that you showed up unprepared, now you're preventing others from listening."

★

The algebra quiz was over. The math teacher collected our notebooks. As I left Kuzmenok was right behind me. He deliberately sat at the last desk so he'd have the same version of the test that I had. I wrote three out of the five problems on a piece of paper and passed it to him.

"Were all those problems exactly right?" he asked me.

"How would I know if they were right or not? I wrote yours the same way I wrote mine. Didn't you do any more of them?"

"Nah. You going to geography?"

"Yes," I said.

"I'm not. I'm going home. I'm gonna get something to eat. You can come with me if you want," he said.

"I don't feel like it."

"Do you have any cigarettes?"

"Yeah," I said.

We went out on the steps and around the corner, then stopped by the beat up side door. I took out my pack of *Stolichnies*—I spent all the money I had on them; I had one kopeck left. We each took a cigarette. I struck a match and lit both of them.

"Give me another one, alright? When I have some more I'll give you some."

"*Astras?*"

"So what if they're *Astras?* All guys smoke them when they don't have much money."

"Like I have so much money. Alright, take one."

Kuzmenok took a cigarette and stuck it in his pocket.

"Shake on it." He stuck out his hand. I shook it. He climbed through the hole in the fence. The porch was dripping. The path was wet. My school slippers and my feet were already wet.

A kid from the first or second grade was running down the hall on the first floor. I grabbed him by the collar of his jacket.

"Listen up, kid. Gimme some kopecks, huh? I don't have enough for a shortbread," I said.

"I don't have any," said the kid.

"And what should I do with you if I find some on you?"

"I don't have any," he said again. I shook him. He pulled himself away. A button tore off his jacket and rolled onto the floor. He ran away and smacked right into the legs of the principal. The principal grabbed him by the ear.

"Don't you know you have to walk when you're inside the school?"

"He was chasing me." The kid pointed his finger at me. I hid behind a column but the principal already saw me.

"Get over here," he said. I went over to him.

"Is this the one that chased you?" he looked at the kid.

"Yes."

"Why were you chasing him? What did you want from him?"

"He wanted to take my kopecks," said the kid.

"He's lying," I said. "I wasn't trying to take anything from him."

"Alright, go on," the director said to the kid. "But look at me—no more running inside the school. Understand? If you do it again we'll be having a different kind of conversation."

He grabbed me by the jacket and led me to his office.

We went inside. The principal closed the door and stood there. On the peeling blue wall there was a wooden box and in it were the keys to all the offices.

"So why is it that I'm having this conversation with you? Why are you demanding money from a first grader? Do you know what that's called? Extortion. His parents give him money for rolls and you want to take it from him? Don't they give you any money at home?"

"They do," I said.

He sniffed me. "I know what it is you squander your money on. What can I say to make you understand what's wrong with what you did?"

"Not a thing."

"You think you're so smart. You know what you can do with your smart mouth?"

"What?" I smirked.

He swung his fist. I ducked. The principal's fist hit the box with the keys. It fell down and the keys hit the floor. The principal brought his fist up to his mouth and licked away some blood, then raised his fist at me again.

"Guys like you are nothing but trouble," he said. "Now, listen.

Go see Sergei Alekseevich to get the tools you need to nail this item back in its place. And if you do a bad job, you will take the blame for it. Got it?"

"Got it," I said. He grabbed me by the shoulder so hard it hurt.

"Answer me the right way."

"Yes."

"That's all," he said. "You can go now."

Kolya pulled his soldering iron out of the rosin box. The rosin was smoking, stinking up the whole room. He was soldering his circuit board.

"What else do you have to do for the director?" he asked.

"Nothing. He's already gone; he went home. I told the cleaning lady she could lock his office, and then I took the tools back down to Alekseevich in the basement. That was it."

Kolya took out his coffee tin and dumped his radio shit on the table. I moved around on the bed to get more comfortable. A snowy sleet was coming down out the window. Kolya pushed the box aside and sighed.

"Are you missing something?" I asked.

"Yeah. My capacitor's not here and I need it."

"Want to walk around?"

"I'm not the type of person you walk around with these days," he said.

"You mean Kuzmenok?"

"Who else would I be talking about?"

"So what's the problem with me walking around with him

sometimes?"

"Nothing. I just don't understand what you have in common with him."

"Why do we have to have something in common? He's just a regular guy. What don't you like about him? That he hit you in the glasses? We were just kids back then, you know, foolish."

"Like he suddenly got smart now or something," Kolya said.

"Well, he's not totally dense like Kosachenko."

"Maybe. You think if you're with him you'll pick up girls, right?"

"I don't think anything."

"I'm telling you, no girl is ever gonna give you the time of day if you're with him. He talks a big game but he's really just a boy. Just like you."

"Oh yeah, and you're not a boy?"

"Well, sure, I'm a boy," he said. "What's wrong with that?"

"Nothing," I said.

The shelf legs scraped across the floor leaving scratches in the paint.

"Lift up a little!" yelled Papa.

I lifted my side of the shelf as much as I could, and we hauled it over to the wall.

"I simply cannot understand why you want it like this," said Mama. "Partitioned off with a bookshelf."

"I want it to be like it's my own room," I said.

"And what a room it is! The shelf is blocking the window so

now it's dark on our side."

"What does it matter to you if it's light?" Papa interjected. "Why don't you turn on the lamp I hung? All it ever does is gather dust."

I went into my "room". My bed was now next to the window, beside the radiator, behind it the shelf had its back to my bed, and next to that was my desk.

I took some posters from my *Melodie und Rhytmus*—Uncle Zhora gave it to me—and started pinning them to the plywood on the back of the shelf.

★

There was a boxing ring in the middle of the gym—a real one with its ropes strung tight. There were footballers at the other end of the gym, a team from the teacher's training institute. Their goalkeeper was training against the ring. He had balls set on both sides of the ring and was working on diving—to one side, and then the other—to save the ball.

"You know you're starting pretty late," the trainer said as he looked at Kuzmenok and me. "These guys have already been at it for half a year. But you can give it a try. I'll show you the stance, and from there everything will depend on your own progress. You might catch up with them or you might not."

The trainer didn't really look like a boxer. He was short and skinny, and he wore glasses.

"Alright, you all need to stretch," he said to the rest of the guys. They lined up along the wall in order of height. "Litvinenko, you lead stretches today."

157

A tall guy in a red t-shirt stepped out of the formation. Kuzmenok and I stood behind the trainer in the corner. He took off his glasses, folded the ear pieces, and hooked one onto the collar of his t-shirt.

"So this is a basic boxing ring," he said. "First you need to learn the right positioning for your feet. In a proper stance, your legs are more important than your hands."

★

K uzmenok and I went up the steps and inside School #28. The zoology teacher had sent us to pick up some flowers during our class. We went down the hall to the door marked "Biology". I knocked. A tall, young teacher opened the door.

"You're from #17, Tatyana Ivanovna's students, yes? Good, now come with me to the greenhouse," she said, then yelled at her class. "Quiet! Don't make any noise!"

It was dirty inside the greenhouse—it appeared to have been watered not long before. The teacher took off her shoes, stuck her feet in a pair of rubber boots, then looked at our footwear. Kuzmenok had on old, shabby shoes, but I had on my new bright blue Czech sneakers. Mama bought them at the October department store for forty-four rubles.

"Maybe you shouldn't go inside the greenhouse," the teacher said to me. "He can come in with me by himself," she nodded at Kuzmenok. "That way you won't soil your nice shoes."

We crossed the street and turned into the courtyard of a two-story building across from School #28. Both of us were carrying flowers wrapped in newspaper. I ended up going inside the greenhouse anyway, and both Kuzmenok's shoes and my sneakers were both smeared with black, runny mud. We wiped them off in some dry grass, but most of the dirt was still there.

"Let's go in the big window store," said Kuzmenok.

"What the hell?" I asked.

"Just to look around."

"What about the flowers?"

"What about the flowers? It's not like they sell those kind of flowers in there," he said.

There was a gray *GAZ-53* van with "BREAD" on it near the big window store. Two red-faced drunk guys were carrying wooden trays filled with squares of black bread into the storeroom.

We went in the store. To the right in the meat department there were pieces of *salo*, liver, and blood sausage in the glass case—beyond that was the dairy section.

"Let's rip off a couple of cheeses," said Kuzmenok.

"What, are you starving or something?"

"Nah, I just want to," he said. He picked up a block of wet cheese in a green and white wrapper and put it in the pocket of his coat.

"Are you pissing yourself?" he asked.

"It's wet. It might leak," I said.

"So what if it's leaks?" he said. I took a cheese too and put it in my pocket. Kuzmenok took another one. "We'll take this one up like we're buying it. You got any money?"

"Just some change."

"Never mind then, we'll just take them," he said. We went up to the cashier.

★

Vaskovskaya from tenth B class went up on stage. She was in her formal school uniform: a dress with a white apron, cuffs, and collars. They probably told her to wear it. She was the student on monitor duty student that evening. Everybody else came in non-school clothes.

"Let's continue our evening of international friendship. Didier Bragda, a visiting student from Chad, will demonstrate a new style of dancing called 'breakdancing'."

Kuzmenok and I sat in the corner against the wall. We had climbed through the window in the toilet on the first floor to get in the school since the event was only for eighth grade and above.

The music came on. A tall black guy with short hair got up from his chair. He was wearing baggy black jeans and a red shirt.

I had seen this "breakdancing" on television, on the show *Sixteen and Up*.[35] The black guy danced similar to what I'd seen on the show, only he didn't spin around on his back. Besides him they had invited fifteen foreigners from the tech college and the teacher's institute to the event—blacks, Arabs, and Vietnamese. After him, two Vietnamese kids sang a song and then two Arabs danced their native dance. Last year Uncle Zhora told me and Natasha that Vietnamese people's favorite dish was fried dog, and that he had tried it when he visited a friend in the teacher's dorm. He said it was tasty, similar to chicken. Natasha screamed and said nothing could ever make her eat dog, even if she was dying of hunger. Uncle

160

Zhora told her she would never guess from the taste that it was dog.

The disco dance was starting. The chairs were all pushed up against the wall. The foreigners danced in their own circle, off to the side. Kuzmenok and I hung around with some guys from eighth A class. Kuzmenok was in their class in first grade but he got held back a year and was assigned to our class.

There was a slow dance. The Vietnamese guy danced with the Vietnamese girls, and one black guy invited Vaskovsakaya to dance. She had changed into jeans and a lilac blouse. He said something to her and she smiled.

There was yelling coming from the corridor. Kuzmenok and I went outside the assembly hall. Timur and the director were holding a black guy, the one who had done the breakdance. Fifteen people were crowded around. Gurlovich from tenth was getting up from the floor. Blood was flowing from his nose. He wiped it with a crumpled handkerchief.

"He went aftah me," the black guy said with an accent. "He's da one dat went aftah me. I'm not da jealous one."

"Go home, go. If you don't know how to behave yourself at a disco dance you'll have to go home." The principal pushed the black guy toward the stairs. "And you." he turned to Gurlovich. "You and I will have our own conversation. Come to my office on Monday."

The math teacher whispered loudly in the German teacher's ear:

"Something's just not right about that, I can't even explain what. I just cannot conceive of one of our girls going to bed with one of them. And you know, they could have a baby that way, a baby! What awaits a child like that in kindergarten or later in school?"

★

Kuzmenok's face was in the peephole. I opened the door.
"You alone?" he asked.

"No," I said.

"Let's go for a walk."

"I have to do my geometry homework."

"Who gives a fuck about geometry? Copy it during the break tomorrow."

"Copy it from who?"

"Somebody. Someone will have it done for sure. The girls always do it."

"Alright, I'll go."

"I'll wait down on the street," he said. "You got any cigarettes? If you do, let me have some."

"Quiet!" I said.

I walked past the mailboxes as I was going down the steps on the first floor. Somebody jumped out from behind the door. I flinched.

"Did you piss yourself?" Kuzmenok cracked up.

We walked out the building's entry. The sky above the kindergarten was pink. The sun had only just gone down. We turned toward building #150. A siren began to wail. Two red fire trucks with flashing lights shot between the buildings. I looked up at Kolya's apartment window.

"Where's that four-eyed friend of yours?" asked Kuzmenok.

162

"How should I know? Maybe he's at home, maybe he's not."

"Fuck him. Anybody who wears glasses is a pussy. You gonna tell me I'm wrong?"

"He's not a pussy," I said.

"Of course he's a pussy," said Kuzmenok. "That's one thing I know for sure."

Andron was standing at the bus stop smoking a cigarette with a filter.

"Ask him for a cigarette," said Kuzmenok.

"He won't give me one," I said.

"Ask him. Are you pissing yourself or something?"

"You ask him."

"I don't feel like smoking," he said. The trolleybus was coming in from Green Meadows. "Let's go downtown, we'll go for a walk."

"What are we gonna do there?"

"You'll see," he said.

"Do you have any trolley tickets?"

"Nope. Who the fuck needs tickets? You scared of the conductor or something?"

We got on the trolleybus. Andron stayed at the stop. He looked at us, threw his cigarette butt on the pavement, and crushed it with his boot.

"We're getting off here," said Kuzmenok.

"Then where are we going?" I asked.

"Sovyetskaya Square. That's where the company club is."

"Which company's club?"

Kuzmenok didn't answer. The trolleybus stopped by the

Buikhovski bazaar. We jumped out, ran across the street and along the Gorky Park fence. There used to be carousels and a Ferris wheel but then they got rid of all of it, and that same year new park opened up on the other side of the Dnieper by the culture center at the chemical complex. All that was left in the old park was the summer theater.

"You know where we'll go? The toilet there has holes in the wall. When the girls go to the toilet at the disco dance in the company club we'll be able to see everything."

"It's not 'the company club'. It's construction firm #9's club," I said.

"All the guys call it the company club. So can we go or are you pissing yourself?"

"Who's pissing himself? I'm not pissing myself."

"The only thing is, there might not be a disco dance today," he said. We went up the building's stone steps. It was built two years ago, along with the monument on Sovyetskaya for the fortieth anniversary of the liberation of Belarus. The club windows weren't lit up and there wasn't any music. The eternal flame was flickering under the sculpture of a babe with wings.

"No disco dance today," said Kuzmenok. "That's too bad. We can't spy on the girls. Do you know how the eternal flame works? How it burns all the time like that and never goes out?"

"There's a pipe with gas running to it. Like the burner on a stove."

"It probably uses a shitload of gas, don't you think?"

"Probably," I said.

"Alright, we'll just go in *GUM* since we came downtown. But there's usually always a disco dance on Saturday at the company club—other days too, but especially on Saturdays. Gangs of guys from different neighborhoods get together in there and kick each other's asses. Worker's comes here too. I'll be coming with them once I start the eighth grade. The guys said I could come with them already, but I told them not until I'm in eighth grade."

★

"Where's your friend?" asked the trainer.

I shrugged.

"That's okay, not a problem. The important thing is that he doesn't miss training. He can miss a birthday."

Ten of us were sitting in the trainer's apartment: one in the armchair, others on the couch and on chairs. Yesterday was Volkov's birthday and the trainer suggested we get together to celebrate. He said they always did that in his club.

We didn't have training that Wednesday. The trainer met us at the bus stop by the *Goods for Men* store. We went in the grocery store and bought two cakes and two big canning jars of orange juice at the cafeteria. The trainer lived on the second floor of a building exactly like ours, also in a two-room apartment, only you had to walk through one room to get to the other. He had sent his wife and kid to the neighbor's. "So they won't disturb us," he said.

I sat on a chair by the window, right under the open transom. Children were chirping like birds in the courtyard, climbing all over the parallel bars, and spreading last year's dead grass all over the place.

"Boxing is really an interesting sport because it's a spectacle," said the trainer. "As it goes in sports, so it goes in life. If a guy is a

165

weightlifter, this is how he how goes around in weightlifting."

The trainer stood up, hunched his shoulders, let his arms hang down and took two big steps. "So he goes in life, so he goes to the store, so he goes everywhere else. A boxer, on the other hand, is always mobile. I would even say graceful. Do you know this word? Do you understand what it means?"

A few of the guys nodded. I took a piece of cake from my plate, had a bite, and sipped some juice, which was in a white cup with the wolf and the rabbit from *I'll Get You!* on it.[36]

"I remember one time at a competition," continued the trainer. "It was the Belorussian Republic student championship. There were plenty of trained boxers who were studying at the various institutes, but there were also guys who were just students. They'd clearly never had any training. There was one guy from the teacher's institute who competed. He was a fellow from out in the country, big and strong. His weight category was eighty-five kilograms. So anyway, when he got in the ring he didn't know the stance or anything. His opponent circled him, jogged in place, got ready to throw a punch. Then, suddenly, this collective farmer takes a wide swing, just like in a country brawl, and beats the guy with one punch. It was a knockout. All the spectators were pissing themselves they were laughing so hard, although it isn't always funny. I know a boxer named Vova Kriptovic who killed a guy in the ring once."

"Did they send him to jail?" asked Litvinenko.

"No, and why would they? He didn't violate any rules, did everything by the book. His opponent just turned out to have a weak heart. Generally speaking, boxing—and really, this is true of any sport—is always a benefit in life. I'm not talking about the obvious things like getting in a fight to defend a girl's honor," the trainer looked at us. "That stuff goes without saying. I'm talking about something else. For example, it made things much easier for me in the army. I graduated from the history department at the Teacher's Institute. They didn't have military classes there so they took me in the army after I already had my diploma. They sent me straight to Pechi, next to Borisov. Have you heard of Pechi? It's a pretty crappy place to be stationed—the regimen there and everything else about it. Our wake-up call was at six o'clock in the morning. I had late classes at the university so I was used to waking up around ten. Anyhow, maybe some of you will have this opportunity."

"Why weren't you assigned to the sports unit?" asked Kostin, a short guy from the Mir-2 neighborhood.

"I have no idea how you get assigned to that one," the trainer picked up his glass and sipped his juice. "But ultimately my situation wasn't any worse. They recognized what a good boxer I was when I was still in Teacher's. Right away the commander told me, let's have you focused on training. Well, I trained, won first place in the unit, then first place in the division. At regionals I got second just as easily. Then that was it—from then until I was discharged, I never once held a gun in my hand or marched in formation—just training and competitions. They let me go home a lot too. The only orders the commander ever gave me were, buy me this in Mogilev, buy me that. But I didn't waste my time looking all over for it—I just bought whatever shit I could find in *GUM*."

"Did you hear about that girl who went to America?" asked Kostin. "Like, she wrote a letter to Reagan or something. A kid from America came here and then this one went over there."

"Katya Lycheva?" I asked.[37]

"I don't care if her name was Lycheva or Gorbacheva, I would totally go to America," he said.

"America probably wouldn't turn anybody away," said the trainer. "America is America."

★

There was half an hour left before training. The gym was still closed, the cloakroom too.

"Let's go inside the institute," suggested Kuzmenok.

We walked up to the second floor, went in the first door, and stood on the balcony overlooking the gym. It was more than twice the size of the one where we had training. There was a real football goal with a net in it under the basketball hoop.

There were students running in the gym for their P. E. class. "I figure they must separate girls and guys for P. E. here," said Kuzmenok.

"Yeah, I know. Natashka told me. Her class is separated too," I said.

A tall, bald guy taught P.E. The students were all wearing shorts and t-shirts, different colors and fashions. Their breasts were bouncing around under their t-shirts as they ran.

"That one's hot, you see her?" Kuzmenok pointed at one with a big chest and butt. "Would you fuck her?"

"Yeah," I said. "Would you?"

"Me too. Who else?"

"That one," I pointed. "And that one. And probably that one."

The P. E. teacher instructed the girls to stop. The students turned their backs to us and started doing stretches. I could see the contours of their panties beneath their shorts.

"Now we will work on sparring," said the trainer. "You, Kuzmenok, you'll spar with Frolov."

"Get ready to see a knockout," Kuzmenok whispered to me. "I'm gonna smack him around like a little puppy."

Frolov was short and compact, almost fat. I didn't know which neighborhood he was from. He was almost always silent. He came to training alone and left alone, almost always, since the first time we went to practice. He wasn't there for Volkov's birthday.

Kuzmenok and Frolov punched each other with their gloves, separated to their corners, then touched gloves again. Kuzmenok threw a right uppercut. Frolov dodged it, threw a hook to Kuzmenok's jaw, a cross to his stomach, and gave him a series of jabs.

Kuzmenok ran back to his corner, danced in place, ran at Frolov again, faked right, jabbed left, then left again. Frolov deflected the blow and crossed to his gut. Kuzmenok gasped and stopped. Frolov punched him full force in the jaw. Kuzmenok crashed down to the oil cloth floor of the ring.

"Knockout!" yelled the guys.

Frolov crawled out of the ring. Somebody patted him on the back. Frolov didn't smile. He wiped sweat from his brow with his glove, which tore open a pimple and spread a little drop of blood. Kuzmenok got up and crawled out of the ring on the other side.

"I guess he totally overpowered him," the trainer looked at Frolov, then at Kuzmenok. "I didn't intend for this to happen. I thought this bout would be an example of equally matched strength. Alright, let's have the next pair get up there."

Kuzmenok and I went to the bus stop. He was still all red. One of his cheeks was swollen. "He got off easy," Kuzmenok said. "That moron trainer had no right to say our match was over. I would have ended him."

"He kicked your ass," I said.

"What? He did not kick my ass, you got that? He just got off easy. And what, you think you kicked Skvortsov's ass?"

"I never said I kicked his ass. He and I had a draw."

"Ours was a draw, too."

"Oh right, a draw," I said.

"Okay, so what if he kicked my ass," he said. "But don't you be blabbing about this at school, alright?"

Mama and Papa were sitting in the kitchen eating sausage patties. Natasha wasn't home.

"Has training been over long?" asked Mama.

"Forty minutes ago. I've been on my way home since then."

"It's best that you come straight home—rather than what you do, goofing around out there all evening. The result of that business is evident in your grade book. All threes and a zero in conduct for the week. I cannot fathom why he signed up for boxing," she said to Papa.

"Boxing is a good idea," said Papa. "A fellow must learn to stand up for himself. I support him on this one."

"It's fine so long as it doesn't interrupt his studies. Only a few

170

months left until the end of the year, and you have so many threes to fix."

"I'll fix them," I said. "You don't need to worry about that."

"We're not worried about anything. You're the one who should be worried, that you'll end up with threes this year."

"I could care less."

"Seriously? What would make you say that?" Mama said. "You could care less about your progress report?"

"Progress reports don't mean anything. Natasha only got three fours and the rest fives, didn't she? And then at the institute she got all threes."

"This conversation isn't about her, it's about you."

"Quiet, listen to what they're saying!" Papa got up and turned up the radio.

"...an accident at the Chernobyl nuclear power station," said the announcer. "There were two deaths as a result of the explosion at the second reactor, as well as a few isolated occurrences of background radiation."

The school's parade formation walked down Peace Avenue, passed the school supply store, and the Enlightenment bookstore and Sausages, crossed at the end of First of May, and came out on Lenin Square. The portraits hung from the sixth floor of the House of Soviets: Marx, Engels, and Lenin. Engels' head was very small and Lenin's was very big. On the side with the portraits, starting on the second-to-last floor, there was red material draped from the windows. Below it, on the Lenin Square side, there were

171

even more portraits. The first one on the right was Gorbachev, the rest I didn't know.

Once Papa took me with him to a parade when I was little, but we didn't stand with the formation from his factory, we just walked. One time we saw the *GUM* women's brass band walking on First of May Street, all of them in yellow hats with black stripes, white shirts, blue skirts and yellow high-heeled boots. Their hairstyles were the only things different about them: some had ponytails, some were just long, and a few had theirs cut short.

★

Dolgobrodov said to Timur, "I called my sister in Dniepropetrovsk. She said there's already a panic there because of the emergency at the power station. Supposedly it wasn't just two men who died but several dozen and there's serious nuclear contamination."[38]

"I was listening to *Voice of America*—on there they said the radioactive cloud is moving across Europe, meaning we might already be covered in it."

"What does that mean?"

"That means that we really shouldn't have gone outside today for the parade, especially with the school children. But everything's always like this. We only ever have serious conversations about things like perestroika and democracy..."

"Alright, alright, you don't need to yell about it. Especially around the pupils."

"You think they don't understand anything? They're grown up

enough to get it already."

★

I woke up. It was slimy and wet inside my shorts. My dick was hard. I had been dreaming that I was sitting in the cloakroom with Shaturo and Voronkova and that I touched Voronkova's breast. It was cloudy out the window. It had probably rained during the night. The rails on the balcony were wet. Drops were hanging from the antenna wires. Far away, behind the houses, a train passed through. The radio was playing in the kitchen:

> Today is Victory Day
> The scent of gunpowder
> Permeates this holiday
> With gray hair in our whiskers
> We will find joy
> With tears in our eyes
> Victory Day!
> Victory Day!
> Victory Day!

★

It smelled like lilacs. There were bushes across from the work-shops. The little kids had picked branches with flowers on them and brought them inside the school. The flowers fell all over the floor in the hallway. Kuzmenok and I were sitting on the back steps. We were ditching geometry.

"There's training today," I said. "You going?"

"No way," he said. "Fuck boxing. It's bullshit. Some guys never do any boxing and they kick more ass than anybody. Are you going?"

"I don't know."

"Wanna play *Choo*?"

I nodded and put my briefcase down on the steps.

"My shake," he said. He gathered up both of our kopecks in his palm, covered them with his other palm and shook them a few times.

"*Choo!*" I said.

Kuzmenok opened his hands. Kopecks fell down on my briefcase. He picked up the coins that landed heads up, using the five-kopeck to knock the fifteen, turning it over from tails to heads. Then he put all the coins in his pocket.

"You cheated," I said. "You helped yourself win with your fingers."

"Get the fuck out of here," he said. "I didn't touch it with my fingers, it turned itself over."

"You get the fuck out of here. You helped it with your fingers. You cheated the other time, too."

"You're the one who cheated. You can go fuck yourself, you got that?"

"You go fuck yourself. I don't want to play with you anymore."

"Like I want to play with you. Take your kopecks."

"You mean the ones you took already?"

"Those are already done. I won them. You trying to say I cheated on those?"

"Wait a minute, how did you win those? You took yours and I took mine. Seriously, am I wrong?"

"Hell no. What's played is played. All these are already mine. If you want you can take the ones that were yours from these."

"Alright," I said.

"My shake," he said. I didn't say anything but I wasn't happy. The point of the game was to get as many coins heads up as you could, and the one who "shook" took all the coins that landed heads up. That guy also had first stab at trying to turn the ones that were left from tails to heads by knocking them with the biggest coin.

Kuzmenok gathered up both of our kopecks in his hands and shook. He opened his hands and the kopecks fell down on my briefcase again. He picked up some coins and put them into his pocket, then he knocked the fifteen with a five-kopeck, trying to turn it over. When that didn't work, he helped it turn over with his finger. He put the fifteen in his pocket as well.

"You cheated again," I said. "I saw it all, you helped yourself win with your finger again."

"Get the fuck out of here," he said. "I didn't touch it with my finger."

"You get the fuck out of here. You helped it with your finger. You cheated the other time, too."

"You're the cheater, and go fuck yourself."

"You go fuck yourself," I said. "This game is over. You take your kopecks and I take mine." I took my fifteen and two twos. Kuzmenok put all the rest in his pocket and walked over to the goal.

I went over to the horizontal bars, took off my jacket, hung by my hands from the biggest bar, and started doing pull-ups. One, two, three... Ten, eleven, twelve... That was all I could do. I jumped down from the bar.

I took the *Komsomolskaya Pravda* and the *Prospective Worker* magazine out of the mailbox.[39] Natasha subscribed to *Prospective Worker*. Kondratevna from the second floor was coming up from below. Mama said she used to work at our school as the biology teacher before she got her pension but that was before my time.

"Hello," I said.

"Hello, little Igor. How are you doing? How are your future relatives?"

"What future relatives?"

"What relatives? You didn't know?" she asked. "You didn't know your Natasha is getting married?"

"No, I didn't know," I said.

"Are they really coming?" I asked Kuzmenok. We sat under the Worker's bus stop shack, chewing on black sunflower seeds, and spitting the shells to the ground.

"They're coming," he said. "If I say they're coming, it means they're coming."

"What time?"

"Seven."

"Won't they be studying for exams? The eighth and tenth grades finished their classes yesterday so they could start studying."

"What exams? Nobody in those grades studies for exams, even honor students. Everybody just goes for walks."

"What should we do with them?"

"What do you think we should do with them? Walk around Worker's, then go to somebody's house and fuck. Is your place free?"

"No."

"That sucks. And my mama is at home. Maybe one of them will have a place to go."

"They won't do that. They won't let us go all the way the first time. We hardly even know them."

"You think they're role models or something?"

"I don't think anything," I said.

"Anyway," he said.

I looked at my watch. It was half past seven. Shaturo and Voronkova weren't there. While we were sitting there, three #2 trolleybuses and two regular buses went past: a #64 "Mogilev-Selets" and a #1 "Green Meadow-Zalutsky Street".

"They're not coming," I said. "If they aren't here by now it means they aren't coming."

"I know that, I don't need you to tell me!" Kuzmenok yelled at me.

"Why are you going all psycho on me? Like it was me who talked to them? Like I'm the one they told they'd meet us?"

"What difference does it make who they promised? I'm gonna have a talk with those bitches."

"Yeah? And what are you gonna do to them?"

"You'll see."

"Alright," I said. "Now what should we do?"

"We can go downtown," he said.

"What's there?"

"I don't know. We can walk around, maybe find some girls to

177

hook up with."

"You say that every time but we never hook up with anybody. You're always too big of a pussy to go up to them."

"You're the one who's a pussy, you got that? I feel like punching you in the face."

"Whatever, fuck it, go where you want by yourself. Go downtown if you want, or go out to Buinichi village." I got up from the bench and walked toward the school.

A trolleybus caught up with me on the other side of the crosswalk. Kuzmenok was sitting in the front seat. He wasn't looking toward the side I was on. I turned toward the school and noticed Shaturo and Voronkova across from the general store. I waved. They stopped. I walked over to them.

"Hi," I said. They both said "hi" to me. "Why didn't you show up?" I asked them.

"Where?" said Shaturo.

"Kuzmenok said—"

They looked at each other and cracked up.

"Why would we tell your friend Kuzmenok that?" said Voronkova. "He's a moron and a freak."

"Totally," Shaturo scrunched up her nose. "You shouldn't hang around so much with that idiot. It's your own business, of course, but if you want a girlfriend—"

"You can walk around with whoever you want, just not with him," said Voronkova.

"What were you doing, going for a walk?" I asked.

"You saw us. What did it look like we were doing?" Shaturo smiled. "Got any smokes?"

"Just two."

"You'll share them with us, of course?"

"Maybe."

"Let's go somewhere. How about the kindergarten?"

"#51?" I asked.

"No, the one that's by the store in Worker's," said Voronkova.

We sat down on the children's carousel. I pushed off from the ground with my foot and the carousel went around, but not very fast. Shaturo inhaled then gave me the cigarette.

"What are you doing this summer?" she asked me.

"I still don't know. Nothing really. You?"

"I'm going to stay with my auntie in Krivoi Rog," said Voronkova. "That's not very far from the sea. They take their *Moskvich* every year to the seaside. I went with them last year too."

"And you?" I turned and looked at Shaturo.

She shrugged. An old *Moskvich-401* drove down the street. A stray dog ran behind it barking. I stopped pushing. The carousel stopped.

It was raining. Thundering. Drops were streaking down the window glass. Natasha was at the table recopying some notes. I sat in the armchair flipping through the *Prospective Worker*. The radio was playing in the kitchen—Kuzmin and Pugacheva's song "Two Stars":

Two stars, two bright spots comprise
My love, like weightlessness.

"Is it true you're getting married?" I asked.

"Who told you? Mama?"

"No, Kondratevna. Mama knows too?"

"What do you think, Kondratevna knows but Mama doesn't?"

"No, but how am I supposed to know who knows? You didn't say anything to me. You think I'm just a little kid, like I won't understand any of it."

"Nobody thinks that," she said. "I don't, at least. I was going to tell you when everybody else found out."

"Who is he?"

"A guy from my class at the Institute. Zhenya Lutsevich. One of the army students."

"What does that mean, army students?"

"He already completed his army service and now he's going to the institute."

"Why hasn't he ever visited us? Lesha was with you all the time," I said.

"He was serving in the Far East. Now he lives with his parents way out by the silicate factory," she said.

Lightning flashed above the school.

I opened the last page of my grade book with the progress report for the quarter and grades for the year. I had three fives for the year: zoology, shop, and physics, and all the rest were fours. Kuzmenok hid his grade book right away—didn't show me. But I knew exactly what he had: all threes except in P.E. and shop, and a two in algebra for the third quarter.

Kuzmenok took out a pack of *Astras*. He and I lit up. Fallen petals were scattered on the grass under the apple tree.

"I'm leaving for the countryside tomorrow," said Kuzmenok.

"For how long?" I asked.

"All summer. Wanna go for a walk tonight?"

"I don't feel like it."

"What are you gonna do?"

"Watch football. It's the World Cup."

"That's not today, it's tomorrow. Isn't it?"

"I think it's today," I said.

Kids from the after school program were racing around on the playground asphalt. Or maybe the school's summer camp was already going. Two teachers were gabbing nearby—a young one and an old one. The young one had a big, round butt and was wearing pink pants, the kind with the legs shaped like bananas.

From the door I could hear unfamiliar voices. I took off my sneakers and looked in the living room. A man, a lady, and a younger guy were sitting on the couch. Natasha was sitting in a chair, Mama next to her in the armchair. The football game had already started on television: USSR vs. France.

"We should get to know each other. This is our youngest, Igor," said Mama. "And this is Zhenya, Natasha's fiancé, and his parents, Olga Sergeevna and Anatoly Sergeevich."

"Hello," I said. Zhenya looked up from the screen, gave me a nod, and went back to watching football. His folks smiled.

"Hello, hello!" said the lady. The guy gave me a nod. Zhenya's cheeks had acne scars, and his greasy hair was speckled with dandruff. He was in plain gray pants and a white t-shirt that said "SPORT."

I sat in a free chair.

"What's the score?" I asked.

"Nil-nil," answered Zhenya.

"I really like Platini," said his mama. "Everybody's always talking about Maradona this, Maradona that. But then he never does anything spectacular. But Platini, well, he's another story."[40]

"I don't have one good thing to say about him," his papa interrupted her. His voice was loud and harsh. "Our boys are gonna win for sure, and then you won't be singing me the praises of that Frenchie Platini."

"Alright, let's change the subject," said Zhenya's mama. "I see you have a shelving unit too, the same one as ours. Only ours has the finished wood. But you were actually smart to get the unfinished one. Now that I see yours, I think the unfinished wood looks better. Don't you think, Tolik? The finish on ours is so light, it looks like it's all faded."

"What are you harping on about?" Zhenya's papa interrupted her again. "Now you're obsessed with a shelving unit. We have business to discuss—where to have the wedding and when, and she's going on about on about shelving units."

"We don't want to have a wedding," said Natasha.

"You don't want to have a wedding? I'm not understanding something here," Zhenya's papa said.

"We don't like the way people always do weddings."

"I am just not understanding something here. Have you completely lost your mind? Not have a wedding! What will people say? Have you thought this through? Zhenya is our only child. What will the neighbors say and all of our relatives? If they hear you got married without having a wedding?"

"Goal!" hollered Zhenya, slapping his palms on his knees.

"Serves those shitty Frenchies right," said his father, smiling. "Who scored?"

"Ratz."

"Why is everything football, football, football now?" said Zhenya's mama. "Football is the least of our worries. They just said they're not having a wedding."

"Don't even listen to them. We decide how it's going to be. Isn't that right?" Zhenya's papa looked at Mama. "We'll do what we have to do so as not to disgrace ourselves. We don't need to have a hundred people of course, but fifty for sure—most likely at the Dnieper restaurant. I have a friend who works there."

"Maybe we could let the kids decide for themselves," Mama said.

"Decide what? About the wedding? Parents plan weddings and we're the parents. That means it's ours to decide. Whatever we decide will be just fine."

The doorbell buzzed.

"That's probably the father of the bride," said Zhenya's mama.

I got up, went to the entry, and opened the door without looking in the peephole. Uncle Zhora was standing in the doorway. It hadn't been very long since he'd reconciled with Papa, and before that he hadn't come over for more than a year.

"Hi," he said.

"Hi," I said.

"We have company," I whispered.

"Company? Who?"

"Zhenya's parents. He's Natasha's fiancé."

"Have I come at a bad time?"

"Of course not, everything's fine."

Uncle Zhora took off his sneakers and went in the living room.

"This is my brother Georgi," said Mama.

"We thought it might finally be your husband," Zhenya's mama turned to the television. The French were hugging on the screen.

"What's going on with football?" asked Uncle Zhora.

"One-one," I said. "The French just scored an equalizer."

"That's how it should be, really," said Uncle Zhora. "The French have a stronger team than we do overall. Our national team is incapable of professional sportsmanship—categorically incapable. They only step it up when they're in the right mood."

"How can you say such a thing?" said Zhenya's papa. "Didn't you see them play Hungary? The pounding our boys gave them there? Smacked them around like little puppies."

"But that's Hungary—you'll agree with me they're not a real team. I have to say my prognosis is pessimistic: our boys won't go any further than the quarterfinals. They just can't make it."

"We'll see, we'll see," said Zhenya's papa. Everybody except Natasha was looking at the screen. Natasha was examining her fingernails. They were painted with red polish but the polish was starting to come off.

"So what are we going to do about the wedding?" asked Zhenya's mama.

★

184

Kovalchuk from seventh B class was standing in the goal and hopping around in place.

"I am Nery Pumpido!"[41]

"You are Nery Pumpkin-fag," said Guron.

The rest of the guys cracked up. There were ten guys from my school in the school courtyard, as well as Guron and German from #28.

"Let's do a penalty shootout!" Guron suggested. "He can be the goalie if he wants to and we'll take turns shooting on him. Three times each. Anybody who doesn't get one in will be eliminated, and the rest will progress to the semi-finals, then the finals and so on."

"Everybody has to pick a country," said Shcherba. "I'm Brazil."

"You want what you can't have, of course," Guron smirked at Shcherba. "I want Brazil."

"Too late. You snooze, you lose."

"Alright, I'm Argentina," said Guron. "Who else is who?"

I picked up the ball and walked over to the penalty mark, which was drawn in the dirt with a rock. The whole field was trampled, there was only one patch of green grass behind the goal.

"What country?" screamed Guron.

"Spain," I said.

"Spain already got eliminated, didn't it? Oh yeah, I guess not. But, you're totally gonna be eliminated on this one."

I moved way back, then ran up and kicked, my foot landing directly under the ball without much force. The ball traveled in an arc and flew right into Kovalchuk's hands. He grabbed it and jumped for joy, like he had stopped a powerful hit.

Guron was sitting behind the goal, flipping through a notebook with a gray cover and grinning. I walked over to him.

"What do you have there?" I asked.

"You're still too young to read this stuff. Not for children under sixteen," he cracked up.

"Come on, give it to the kid. Give him a chance to spank his monkey," said German. He was hanging on the goal's crossbar, a cigarette smoking away in his mouth.

"Maybe he already spanks his monkey? How would you know?" said Guron. "Alright, enough bullshit. What are you gonna give me as a deposit?"

"First you tell me what it is. Maybe it's something I don't need."

"You need it, kid. Every guy needs it. You're gonna read it, then you're gonna jerk off, and then you'll start chasing girls and begging them to let you stick your dick in them. They'll tell you to fuck off—and then ask guys like us to kick your ass," German said. He and Guron cracked up.

"I can give you my watch," I said. I unfastened my watchband and took it off.

"That watch is shit," said Guron. "But the watchband isn't half bad. Okay, give it back to me in two days. German only just gave it to me. I just started reading it myself."

I gave Guron my watch and took the notebook.

"Are we gonna play football today or what?" he yelled. "Let's pick teams."

★

186

The dusty light bulb was glowing above the door. Water was running noisily through the pipes. Somebody—upstairs, downstairs, or on our floor—coughed loudly. I was sitting on the pot reading a story from Guron's notebook:

"...then he pulled out of her. A trickle of jizz splashed on the bed sheet."

My dick was hard. I pulled down my shorts and blue sweatpants, touched it, squeezed it. I'd never seen how you're supposed to jerk off, but right away I understood what I had to do. I wrapped my hand around it and moved it up and down. After a few jerks it started to feel nice. I moved my hand faster. A few drops of something cloudy and white flowed out. I kept jerking off. Suddenly the joy hit and everything went dark before my eyes. A drop of jizz was hanging on the door along with the dried drips of white paint. I jerked a few more times but my hand hurt. I unwound some toilet paper from the roll, wiped my dick and the door, put the paper in the pot, and flushed. Upstairs or downstairs somebody coughed again. I got up from the pot and put the notebook on the tank. My dick was still hard. I pushed it down with the elastic of my shorts so it wouldn't stand out and stepped out of the toilet.

"Why were you sitting in there so long? Do you have a stomach ache or something?" Mama yelled from the bedroom.

"No, everything's fine."

I went into the bathroom and turned on the cold water. The hot had been off for three weeks because the hot water pipe in the courtyard was all dug up.

★

Natasha came out of the living room in a white dress with red flowers on it. She was holding a knapsack with a picture of Alla Pugacheva on it.

"You're going out?" I asked.

"Yeah, Zhenya and I are going to the beach."

"Sacred Lake?"

"No, on the Dnieper."

"Sacred would probably be better. There isn't a current to worry about there."

"It's not bad on the Dnieper."

"Are you going to live with us or them?" I asked.

"Them," she said.

"How many rooms do they have?"

"Two, like us. But they're closer to the institute. Of course I'd rather stay at our place. You know, I really can't stand his parents. I don't know why. But there's nothing I can do about it. Know what I mean?"

"What does he think of Mama and Papa?"

"What do you mean?"

"Well, you can't stand them but does Zhenya like our mama and papa?"

"I don't know. He doesn't really have any basis for judgment. They only saw each other the one time. He practically never even saw Papa, Papa got there so late. It's a good thing he was sober."

"Almost sober."

"Well, yeah," she said.

"What if he changes his mind and you guys can live here?" I asked.

"That probably won't happen. But this is a positive change for you. You'll have your own room when I leave."

"True, yeah, but it doesn't matter to me."

"Alright, I need to go," she said. "I'm meeting Zhenya at the bus stop at half past."

★

Uncle Zhora took out a bottle of *Zhigulevskoye* and poured some beer in his glass and mine. We were sitting on a couple of folding stools on his dorm balcony. Everyone's room opened onto the same shared balcony, and it looked out over Cosmonaut Square. There was a crane towering over the square—a building was under construction on the other side, three of its floors already complete.

Uncle Zhora took a long swig, downing half the glass. I took a drink, then set my glass down on the on the balcony's stone floor.

"How's your sister doing?" he asked.

"Alright. She didn't get any threes this semester."

"And what does she think about her upcoming event? Is she ready?"

"What does she have to do to get ready? I don't know. She and Zhenya went to the Dnieper today."

"Matrimony is always a complicated affair," Uncle Zhora said. "Everything seems easy and wonderful in the beginning. And then it begins, the tangled mess of relationships—fathers-in-law, mothers-in law, all of that stuff. I'm speaking frankly here, from my own experience. I've yet to encounter a situation in which both the father-in-law and mother-in-law love the bride. It's all on a subconscious level and there's nothing you can do about it. They can, well, not love, but at least respect a son-in-law. But not a daughter-in-law."

"You mean they hate Natasha already?"

"You know, first of all, we need to hope for the best, because for all we know they may be the exception to the rule. And second, this is simply the objective reality we live in. For example, you and I live in the country with the title USSR, and this country is objectively worse than the country with the title USA and the country called the Federal Republic of West Germany. Even our rulers are gradually beginning to recognize this. So what does it all mean? It means we have two paths to choose from, strictly speaking. Either try to leave the USSR and go to the USA or the FRG—but the chance of being able to do this is small, practically zero. Our other option is to live here and adapt to the circumstances of our reality. Or don't adapt to society's circumstances, but operate in defiance of those circumstances, while still keeping them in mind, that is. And as it goes in life, so it goes in matrimony—it's roughly the same concept, just a more specific, concrete example of it. Look, there's a new *Moskvich* down there—a *2141*. They released that model this year to coincide with the opening of the 26th Party Congress. But it's still just a *Moskvich*. You can put a coat of paint on a piece of shit, and the paint may well be pretty, but it will stink just the same."

I picked up my glass and took a swig. Uncle Zhora pulled out a pack of *Orbits*, took out a cigarette, and clicked his lighter.

"I heard a joke not too long ago," he inhaled, blew out the smoke, and finished off his beer. "It's a lot like real life and it could apply to many of my students. I think it applies to quite a few in your class as well. So they decide to have a competition between students with twos from Soviet schools and some monkeys. One monkey goes right up to a tree with bananas hanging from it. He looks up, reaches for a branch, and starts to shake it, but the bananas don't fall. They say to the monkey, think it through! The monkey thinks, takes a stick, and hits the bananas with the stick. Then they give the very same assignment to a student who gets twos. He shakes the branch and the banana doesn't fall, so they tell him the same thing: think it through! And the two student says, what's there to think about? I must shake the tree!

★

Our entire courtyard was visible from the gazebo, our building too. There were bed sheets hanging on our balcony. Yakimovich was smoking on the fourth floor. A yellow *Moskvich* was parked by the entry.

German took out a bottle of Azerbaizhani port and tore away the plastic court with a pocket knife. The cork rolled away under the bench.

"Couldn't they kick us out of the kindergarten?" I asked.

"Who would do that?" Guron looked at me like I was an idiot.

"Well, the guard or somebody."

"The guard is Kuzmich, he's our man. If he comes around we'll just give him some booze."

"Alright kid, time for your first," German gave me bottle. "But for god's sake not a big one."

I took a swig. The wine didn't taste very good, it was bitter, but I didn't let it show. Guron took the bottle from me.

"So, did you jerk off?" German nodded at the notebook. I had only just handed it back to Guron. I shook my head.

"I don't believe you. Every guy jerks off when he reads something like this. Tell the truth, did you jerk off or not?"

Guron took a good swig and gave the bottle to German.

"Just for that we'll beat the shit out of you now," he said. "Isn't that right, German?"

They both cracked up.

"Alright, then to hell with you. You don't know how good you have it. You just don't want to tell the truth, and you don't have to." German took a sip from the bottle and set it down on the grungy gazebo floor. "If you'd have told the truth we would've taken you with us to find some girls. But you didn't, so we won't."

"Don't feed him that crap, German. We still wouldn't have taken him with us," said Guron. "He would have done something stupid and the girls would have laughed at us. Like, what did they bring that kid along for, he's such a loser! We shouldn't really give him any more, should we, German?"

"That's enough shit talk about the kid," said German. "Now he's crying."

"Piss off. I'm not fucking crying! We'll see which one of us is gonna cry!"

"Okay kid, show us what you're made of," said Guron. "Hit it again. German, pass him the bottle!"

German took a swig and gave me the bottle. It was already more than half empty. I nodded and took a sip, just barely managing to keep from spitting it out.

Guron drop-kicked the empty bottle. It rolled away on the wooden floor.

"Kid, what do you think, if I punched you right now do you

think you could stay on your feet?" asked German.

"And if I punched you right now, German you think maybe you'd fall over?" I said.

Guron cracked up. German threatened to hit me but Guron grabbed him.

"Don't you touch the kid," he said. "Can't you see he's drunk? He doesn't need much, all he has to do is catch a whiff of the cork and he's loaded."

"Maybe you're the one who's, like, loaded—or whatever. I'm totally like, always, like—this is normal for me." I was slurring my words. German and Guron both cracked up. "Kiss my ass, faggots. What are you laughing at?"

They kept laughing. "You can both fuck off, I'm leaving," I said.

Guron grabbed me by the neck ad squeezed hard. "Don't you ever leave your brothers with a 'fuck off', you got that? If you're just fucking around, well, then just maybe that's alright, but never a real fuck off, got it? They won't stop to see if you're drunk, they'll just beat the shit out of you and that will be that. Alright, get out of here. I've got things to discuss with German. Hey, where you going? Leave the notebook."

I set the notebook on the bench.

"So you liked it, right?" German giggled. "How long before you're gonna stick your dick in a babe? Ten years or so, yeah? You should jerk off every day until then. Get yourself off!"

Mama was the only one home. She was sitting in the living room on the couch.

"Hi," I said.

"Hi," she said. "Oh my, have you been drinking?"

"So what if I was?"

"What do you mean, so what? How old are you? You're only fourteen. You're a growing boy. Where were you drinking? With whom and what?"

"None of your business!"

"What did you say to me? What do you mean, none of my business?"

"Whether I was drinking or not. It's none of your business."

"What do you mean, none of my business? I'm still your mother, aren't I? I am not going to tolerate you drinking at such a young age."

"You don't need to lecture me, alright? All you say is 'drinking's bad, drinking's bad.' What's so bad about it? Papa drinks, Uncle Zhora drinks," I said.

"Papa gets drunk sometimes and Uncle Zhora too. But neither one is an alcoholic. And they didn't drink when they were your age," she said.

"How do you know? Maybe they got loaded in the first grade," I laughed.

"Go to bed. There's no point in having this conversation with you tonight. We'll talk about this tomorrow."

Mama turned back to the television. There were two performers standing on a big stage, a lady and a guy.

"Welcome to our show!" the lady said and smiled.

"Good evening, my friends!" said the guy. "Let's get right to our singing competition."

★

194

I took my hidden pack of *Kosmos* out from under the tin ledge on the balcony, struck a match, lit up, and took a drag. It was dark. The sky over Kindergarten #51 was still light. The leaves on the trees shaded half the courtyard. Over by the third entrance next to where the hot water pipes were dug up there was a big piece of earth dug out by the excavator. I lifted my head and looked up. Olka Yakimovich's head was peeping out from the fourth floor balcony.

"Look, Manenok won't let that girl through the entry," said Olka.

I moved so I could see around the potted pansies. On the porch of the entry under the lamp stood Sergei Manenok, younger brother of Sanya, the one who got killed in Afghanistan. With him was some babe I didn't know. He was holding the entry door shut and blocking her path. She had on jeans—not worn ones, almost new—and a white t-shirt. On her back, under her shirt, I could make out the clasp of her bra.

"You're not all that, you know?" said Manenok. "I'm not gonna do anything to you, I just want to talk to you."

"I don't have anything to say to you."

"How come you don't have anything to say to me, huh? Who do you think you are? Tell me that—who do you think you are?"

She took a step back and stood there. Manenok looked at her like an idiot.

"So what, we're just gonna stand here?" he asked. She was silent.

I took one last inhale, then flicked my butt at Manenok and sat back down so he wouldn't notice it was me.

"Who was that? Suck my dick!" I could hear Manenok holler. "You trying to fuck with me? Flicking butts at me—you're lucky you didn't set my polo shirt on fire. If I find out who did that, I'll fucking cut you!"

The building's entry door slammed. There were footsteps. Then the door slammed again. I looked down cautiously. Manenok was standing by the entry. The girl was already gone. He took a pack of *Astras* out of his pocket and started smoking as he walked toward building #150. Just below on the second floor, the light was on in the kitchen window below our apartment. It was the girl.

From where I stood I could see her open the refrigerator, take out a bottle of cream, push her fingers through the lid, and pour some. She was probably a relative of Auntie Sveta's. Auntie Sveta lived alone with her son Vitya. He graduated from School #28 and went to the engineering institute, but last year he got sent away to the army.

The courtyard lit up from the headlights of a car. A *Volga* sped quickly away from building #146. It stopped by the fourth entrance.

★

I was standing on the balcony—waiting for her to come out on her balcony. Swallows were darting back and forth above the building. Little kids were squealing at the kindergarten. Motors were roaring at the engine repair factory. The sun still hadn't risen on our side and half the courtyard was in the shadow of the building. In the morning I'd seen her in the window of her kitchen. She took the butter dish out of the refrigerator and spread butter on a baguette, then put the kettle on.

Kolya was walking down the road, probably coming from the big window store. He was carrying a three-liter bottle of kvas, two bottles of milk, and a square loaf of bread in a net bag. We hadn't seen each other since the start of the summer vacation. I whistled. He looked up. "Hi," I said.

"Hi."

"How are things?"

"The usual. Vacation's really boring."

"How's your brother?"

"He's serving in Afghanistan."

"Alright, well, see you later," I said.

"Bye," he said.

She stepped out on her balcony. I jumped a little. It felt like something exploded inside of me. She was in the same white t-shirt as yesterday and red sweatpants. She put her hands on the balcony railing, looked to the side, then looked up. I didn't have time to hide.

"Hi. I'm Ira," she said. "What's your name?"

"Igor."

"Nice to meet you."

"You too. Are you a relative of Auntie Sveta?"

"I'm her niece."

"How long ago have you been here?"

"Three days."

"Where are you from, if it's not a secret?"

"It's not a secret. I'm from Leningrad. Listen, do you have anything for playing tapes? I brought a few tapes with me and Vitya's tape deck—that's Auntie Sveta's son, you probably know him—it's not working. So I don't have any way to listen to them," she said.

"Yeah, we have a tape player."

"Then maybe I could come up to your place, if you don't mind."

"No, sure, I don't mind," I said.

I'd never heard this song before, but I liked it:

Take me to the river,
Put me in the water,
Teach me the art of silence.

"It's a group called Aquarium," said Ira.[42] "They're from my city, from Leningrad. A lot of people are listening to them right now."

"Why haven't you ever visited your aunt before?" I asked her.

"My parents split up when I was six, and Papa moved north so we hardly ever even associated with him. And Auntie Sveta is his sister. It was maybe half a year ago that he came back to Leningrad, and we started seeing him again. So anyway, he offered to send me to visit Auntie Sveta for a month. At first Mama didn't want to let me come, but we don't really have any relatives anywhere else. Mama was the only child in her family. My grandfather, her papa, died not too long ago, and my babushka also lives in Leningrad. I've never been out of the city. Well, only on excursions with my class, but never to visit family."

"Do you like it here?"

"It's hard to say. Can I be honest? Not really—too many freaks around here. You know what we call guys like that? *Gopniki*.[43] Are they called that here, too?"

"I've never heard that word before."

198

"Well, all the same, you know which people I'm talking about." She looked her little digital watch. "You know what? I have to go. I promised my aunt I'd get dinner ready. She'll probably be home soon. But I'll leave the tapes if you want."

"Yeah, leave them," I said. "That would be great."

★

The door shut in the entryway. Natasha and Zhenya came in. I looked out from the living room. They had a box and a paper bag from the bridal shop. The registry office had given them coupons in case there was something they still needed to buy for the wedding.

"What did you buy?" I asked.

"I got a pair of sandals. Zhenya got shoes but he still needs a shirt and tie," said Natasha.

They came in the living room after they took off their shoes and put the box and bag on the couch.

"Do you know the rock group called Aquarium?" I asked them.

"I've heard the name before," answered Natasha.

"That group is prohibited, they're anti-Soviet," said Zhenya. "First semester they showed us a list of prohibited groups we're discouraged from listening to..."

"The Komsomol leaders showed you all the names?" asked Natasha.

"Yeah. I remember some of their names," he said. "German-Polish Aggression, Leather Commissaries, Sewage Pit..."

"Well, Aquarium is a pretty normal name compared to those," said Natasha.

"What difference does their name make if the group is anti-Soviet?" he said.

★

"Hi!" said Ira, and waved at me. She was on her balcony; I was on mine. She had on different things: old, worn jeans and a red t-shirt.

"Hi!" I answered.

"What are you doing?"

"Nothing, really."

"Maybe we could go for a walk together? You could show me your neighborhood, because I've already been here a week and I still haven't walked around."

"Sounds good, let's go," I said.

"I'll wait downstairs by the entrance," she said. "Five minutes, okay?"

We walked around the building on the side with the green grocer.

"Across the street, that's my school," I said.

"Have you always gone there, like since first grade?" she asked.

"Yeah."

"I've been in a new one since seventh. I wasn't very happy in the old one, and I had a problem with one of the teachers. Mama got me transferred to a different school."

We crossed the street but didn't go to the school. We turned at the bus stop and went past the three-story apartment building that had the Beacon bookstore on the ground floor.

"And right there, that used to be a grocery store. It burned down three or four years ago," I said.

"Aren't they going to rebuild it?"

Next to the bread kiosk was a yellow barrel of kvas. The lady selling it was from the first floor of our building.

"Should we have some kvas?" I asked.

"I don't want any," she said.

Some babe was carrying a skinny man in glasses to the bus stop, drunk off his ass. I realized it was my boxing trainer but I didn't say anything to Ira.

The post office and the police substation were on the left, and on the right was the beer hall, the cafeteria, and the deli. Behind the substation was where the streets of single-story country houses started.

"It's kind of like we're out in the country, huh?" I asked.

Ira shrugged. "There are different kinds of neighborhoods in Leningrad, too. We just happen to live in a newer neighborhood not far from the Primorskaya metro. The Gulf of Finland is right there."

"That's cool."

"Honestly, there's nothing cool about it. There's always wind coming in from the gulf so it's almost always cold."

"Is there a big difference between Mogilev and Leningrad?"

"Definitely. People are different here, they dress differently, they talk about different things, and with a Belarusian accent."

"Do I have one?"

"You do. Yours isn't very strong but I do notice it. Plus, people are all the same here. There's more diversity where I live."

"What do you mean, diversity?"

"I mean like the way people look and their clothes are more diverse. But it's not just that. I don't know how to explain it," she said. We walked up to the Green Meadow trolley depot. One trolleybus was parked over the repair pit and another was by the controller's office. "So, shall we go back?" she asked.

I nodded.

"Did I offend you or something?" she said.

"Of course not," I said. "What made you think that?"

We went in the front entrance and up to the landing between the third and second floors. Manenok was coming down from above. "Irka. Hi," he said.

She didn't answer. He stuck his hand out to me so I put mine out. He shook it forcefully—didn't let go. Ira turned and looked at us. I took my hand back. Manenok went down the stairs.

"Who was that?" Ira asked.

"A neighbor from the fifth floor," I said.

"Are you friends with him?"

"No. He's three years older than me. I don't know why he wanted to shake hands today."

"Well, thank you for the tour. It was interesting."

"Really?"

"Yes."

"Well, bye," I said.

"Bye," she said.

★

"I will fuck you up every day," said Manenok. "You got that?" We were standing inside the entry by the mailboxes. The window looked out on the rooftop above the entry. It was thick with green moss and had pieces of broken bottles and crumpled *Prima* cigarette packs scattered around on it. The glass was dirty, and a spider web was hanging between the window frames.

"I will fuck you up every day," Manenok repeated. "If you don't stop bugging her."

"You're the one who's bugging her," I said.

He hit me in nose and then kicked me in the stomach. I winced and squatted down, leaning against the wall under the mailboxes. Manenok went up the stairs. I stood up, squatted again, then stood up again. I'd heard lots of times that you should squat down if you get hit in the stomach or the balls. My stomach muscles released. I put my palm under my nose. There wasn't any blood.

I stood on the balcony waiting for Ira and Auntie Sveta to return. Ira told me they were going to visit one of Auntie Sveta's friends.

It was dark in the bedroom. Mama and Natasha were watching television in the living room.

Papa still hadn't come home.

I didn't feel like jerking off. I jerked off at home after I walked around Worker's with Ira, and it felt disgusting for some reason.

Auntie Sveta and Ira appeared from around the corner on the side with the green grocery. They probably took the trolleybus to the Motor Factory stop. Ira was in a blue t-shirt and jeans. Auntie Sveta was talking:

"And that's why everybody's leaving Kiev right now, they're all getting sick from the radiation. Before it was impossible to get the paperwork you needed to move there. It was a city with limited registration. But it would certainly be easy now because they're all leaving, transferring to other cities..."

They walked in the entry. The door shut.

★

"Igor, go get the mail," said Mama.

I didn't really want to go because I knew I might run into Manenok downstairs by the entrance. I suddenly felt like shitting myself, even though I had just taken a shit like an hour before.

I took the key from the hook above the mirror, poked my feet into my slippers, turned the lock, and went out on the landing and down to the second floor. A lock clicked upstairs. Something lurched in my stomach. I unbolted the box and took out the *Pravda*. Nothing else came on Mondays, just magazines sometimes. Manenok was coming down the stairs.

"Hey kid. Did you think I was just blowing smoke? You didn't understand, huh? Here's what I said: I will fuck you up if you don't leave her alone."

He was wearing sneakers instead of slippers. I wondered if he put them on so he'd be more comfortable if he needed to kick somebody. I put the newspaper on the windowsill. He raised his fist but didn't hit me. I flinched.

"What, you're pissing yourself? Oh yeah, I can see it. You're pissing yourself. You think I should let you go? Nope, I'm not gonna let you go."

He kicked me. I covered my balls with my hand so his foot hit my fingers. It hurt, but not as bad as it would have.

"Why'd you cover it up, huh? Come on, take your hand away."

The door of apartment #39 clicked. Ira looked out.

"What do you want from him?" she asked quietly. "You'd better leave him alone, or else."

"Or else what, huh? You, little girl, better think carefully about who you're talking to, alright? This is my entrance and my neighborhood, so don't be threatening me, alright?" He raised his foot like he was going to kick me. I jumped to the side. "Alright, next time." Manenok said, and went up the stairs.

"Come see me if you want," said Ira. "My aunt is at work."

The apartment was exactly the same as ours, only furnished much differently. The living room was where our bedroom was and vice versa. There was an accordion case on the floor in the corner of the living room. I nodded at it.

"Who plays that?" I asked.

"Vitya used to play, but not for very long. He didn't like music school so he gave up on it. He said he didn't want to and that was that. But I wasn't allowed to do that so I stayed in it until the end. In violin class. Now I can't even stand to look at a violin. There was one good thing—it was music school that got me started listening to classical music. Do you like anything classical?"

"Yeah, I've listened to a little of it. We had to take some music classes in school but none of it was very interesting."

"I didn't like it in school, either. Only when I went to the music school," she said.

"Well, I should probably go," I said. "I was just supposed to get the mail for Mama. Maybe we could walk around the city this evening."

"I can't today. Aunt Sveta's colleague from work is coming over with her daughter today. Let's do it tomorrow."

"Okay, tomorrow. Well, tomorrow my sister's getting married," I thought for a second. "But that's in the afternoon and I'm not going to the restaurant after. Nobody under twenty-one is allowed in there."

Zhenya put the ring on Natasha's finger. He couldn't get it on, so she helped him with her other hand and then put his ring on him. The lady from the wedding registry with the standard red sash across her shoulder was smiling from ear to ear. Natasha and Zhenya kissed. The photographer was a bald guy with a potbelly and a nice *Kiev-4* camera. He clicked a button and the flash went off. They wouldn't let me be the photographer. Zhenya's folks said they had a well-known photographer they could use. At first I was upset, but then I realized it was better this way—if the photographs turned out bad I wouldn't have to feel guilty.

We went outside—Zhenya, Natasha, the folks—ours and his—the photographer, and the witnesses, a guy and a babe from their class at the institute. Nobody else was invited to the registry. Not even Uncle Zhora, but he didn't want to come anyway. He said he'd go to the restaurant but that he hated everything about the registry. There were two cars, a *Lada-6* and a *Lada-3*, decorated only in ribbons, without the traditional two rings and a doll on the hood. A trolleybus went past on First of May Street. The people in the windows turned their heads, gawking at us. Zhenya's papa grabbed his hand and shook it, congratulating him.

"You can go with them if you want," Mama said to me. "There's room in the car. We're going over to the restaurant right now to make sure they set everything up properly."

Zhenya and Natasha stood against the background of the Saltanovka memorial. They built a small white chapel here because there was some battle on this spot in the year 1812. Beyond Saltanovka there was a dangerous stretch of road with sharp turns. It was called "The Mother-in-Law's Tongue".

"Kids, cross over to this side please," the photographer directed them. "The sun's better over here."

I was standing there leaning against the fender of the *Lada-6* with the driver, Zhenya's cousin. We were smoking his *Kosmos*.

★

From the shore on other side of the Dnieper, behind the trees, I could see the culture center at the chemical complex. Long, long ago, before it was even built, I saw a model of it in the regional museum. I went there with Babushka. The museum closed for repairs not long after that and never reopened.

"Where's your building? Over there?" Ira asked, nodding toward the pipes of the Kuibishev factory.

"Yeah, on that side, only further away. You can't see it from here."

We stood in the square around the statue of Gorky in the corner of the park. The park was on a hill from which you could see

207

a great distance: the other side of the Dniper and the Menzhinka neighborhood, the Buikhovski bazaar, a church, and some more wooden houses.

We were alone in the square. Further on, some people were sitting together on a bench along the path. A guy in new jeans was walking down the path.

"I want some new jeans. Mama promised she'd buy me some," I said. "Most likely *FUS*. They sometimes have them in the men's clothing store."

"Where I live they're already selling them everywhere. There's even a billboard in *Gostiny Dvor*, that's our big department store. It says, 'Comfort, Beauty, and Reliability: Jeans.'"

A motorboat drifted past on the Dnieper. Waves began to drift toward the shore.

"Are you gonna kiss me?" Ira said quietly. "Or are you going to wait for, I don't know, how much longer?"

I leaned in and put my hands on the yellow railing, then touched my lips to her lips.

A trolleybus went by below. The wires started wavering.

NOTES

1 Because it was nearby and easily accessible, Odessa was the most popular Black Sea holiday destination for many residents of Belarus, Ukraine, and Russia in the 1980s. The region's tourist infrastructure wasn't well developed, though, so most visitors spent their holidays in substandard accommodations.

2 An oblast is an administrative region in most of the USSR and current Belarus and Russia. It's similar to a county or borough.

3 *Operation Y and Shurik's Other Adventures* was a hit slapstick comedy in 1965. Shurik the protagonist was an awkward student with a knack for stumbling into wacky misadventures.

4 Because jeans were in such demand in the Soviet Union and the availability of imported jeans was limited, Soviet factories manufactured their own knock-offs, most of which looked bad or were made of some non-denim material that didn't fade. All imported jeans were described as 'genuine.' Unlike their locally manufactured counterparts, 'genuine' jeans faded, and this became a commonly used criterion for quality.

5 Around age fourteen, Soviet teenagers were all required to join the communist youth organization Komsomol and wear a pin on their school uniform to signify their membership.

6 Pioneers was a youth communist organization, with mandatory membership for all school children starting around age ten. By the

mid-1980's, membership was mostly a formality and the organization did little actual work.

7 The card game Thousand is popular in several Eastern European countries. The object of the game is to accumulate a score of 1,000 points by bidding for and exchanging cards.

8 The food ration program during Perestroika was part of a last-ditch central planning effort to combat food shortages in the stagnant Soviet economy.

9 Buinichi Field is the site of a brutal battle that took place near Mogilev between the Soviet army and the Nazis, with a combined death toll of more than 100,000. It did in fact take place in 1941, but Igor and Kolya are unsure of their history.

10 Based on the novel by Anatoly Ivanov, the 1970's Soviet television series *Eternal Calling* (*"Vechni Zov"*) followed the lives of a Siberian family through the historically tumultuous period from 1906 to 1960.

11 *GUM* is an acronym for *Glavni Universalni Magazin*, or "Main Department Store". Moscow's *GUM* is a well-known Soviet-era landmark, but many other Soviet cities had and still have a *GUM* as well.

12 The *chelyuskintsi* were the crew of the steamship *Chelyuskin* and important characters in the mythology of Soviet heroism. The SS *Chelyuskin* was designed to navigate the Arctic waters of the Northern Maritime Route without an icebreaker. It ran into trouble and sunk in 1934, but the crew made a miraculous escape and was rescued from the ice by aircraft.

13 Alla Pugacheva was the Soviet Union's most prominent pop diva and is still a popular music icon in the region.

14 Every Soviet community had a standard road sign indicating to cars when they have entered its boundaries. Conversely, an identical sign with a line striking across the community's name was positioned for the view of cars departing the community. These signs remain a tradition in many of the former Soviet republics.

15 In another example of the mythology of Soviet heroism, most Soviet cities had streets and squares named after a specific list of early Soviet leaders including Sergo Ordjonikidze, an official of Georgian ancestry who held significant bureaucratic positions in the 1920's and 1930's.

16 Kvas is a fermented, non-alcoholic drink still popular in many parts of the former Soviet Union.

17 Konstantin Chernenko was the general secretary of the Soviet Union's communist party from February of 1984 until his death on March 10, 1985.

18 Kulak was a derogatory term Soviet authorities used to label and harass affluent farmers who resisted collectivization in the early decades of the Soviet Union.

19 March 8th is International Women's Day.

20 Nikolai Slyunkov was the first secretary of the Belorussian Republic in the 1980's, notorious for his role in suppressing information about the Chernobyl nuclear disaster in neighboring Ukraine, which affected a substantial portion of Belarus.

21 A *blin* (better known by its plural *blini*) is a crepe-like pancake which is often rolled and stuffed with a variety of fillings such as butter or jam.

22 Victory Day was a major holiday that commemorated the Soviet Union's victory over Nazi Germany. It became another significant element of the mythology of Soviet heroism.

23 *Zhigulevskoye* was a common brand of beer brewed throughout the Soviet Union, one of few beers available at that time.

24 *School* by Arkady Gaidar was a semi-autobiographical coming-of-age story set during the 1917 Bolshevik revolution and the civil war that followed it from 1918-1922. The main character was supposed to set an example for young readers to help them choose a life path that would service communist ideals.

25 Shashlik is a Georgian dish similar to a shish kebab that was popular throughout the Soviet Union.

26 *Gosplan* was the Soviet Union's economic central planning committee. It was notorious for its failure to anticipate the population's demand for goods and services (so Igor's father's comment here is ironic).

27 Ivan Franko (1856—1916) was a Ukrainian poet and socialist revolutionary, championed by the Bolsheviks and included in their Communist hero mythology. Streets were named after him all over the Soviet Union, not just in Ukraine, but by the 1980's few people knew who he was.

28 Yuri Andropov was the General Secretary of Communist Party in the Soviet Union from late 1982 until his death in 1984, after

Brezhnev and before Chernenko. As a former KGB chief with a record of suppressing dissent and crushing uprisings, he took a hardline approach to solving the Soviet Union's problems, an approach that was ultimately unsuccessful.

29 Pirozhki are bread buns stuffed with fruits, meats, or vegetables.

30 *Seventeen Moments of Spring* was a classic 1973 TV miniseries about a Soviet spy operating in Nazi Germany at the end of WWII. *The Battle of Moscow* was a less notable WWII film in 1985.

31 *Doktorskaya* was a popular kind of sausage originally developed as a kind of low-fat diet alternative, which is why it was called "doctor's sausage".

32 *The Adventures of Elektronik* was a 1980 TV miniseries for children about a sixth grade boy who meets a robot that looks exactly like him.

33 *Modern Talking* was a German pop music duo in the mid-eighties, and one of few groups from the West that gained notoriety in the Soviet Union.

34 Halley's Comet was visible with the naked eye from Earth in 1986, which only happens once every 75 years.

35 *Sixteen and Up* was a youth TV show that became especially popular during Perestroika when it began to report on youth sub-cultures and other subjects that had been otherwise ignored by the Soviet media.

36 *I'll Get You!* was a classic Soviet cartoon in which a villainous wolf was forever trying to capture the protagonist rabbit.

37 Katya Lycheva was a Soviet schoolgirl who was invited to visit the USA in 1986 in response to an earlier visit to the Soviet Union by American schoolgirl Samantha Smith in 1983. Lycheva's visit was highly-publicized in the Soviet media and she was for a short time a celebrity.

38 Dniepropetrovsk is a major city in eastern Ukraine downstream from Chernobyl on the Dnieper River.

39 *Prospective Worker* magazine was originally a dry magazine aimed at vocational students, but it became popular in the 1980's when it began running articles about popular music and teenage culture.

40 Legendary footballer Diego Maradona was captain for Argentina's team in the 1986 World Cup. Michel Platini captained the French World Cup team that year.

41 Nery Pumpido was the goalkeeper for Argentina in the 1986 World Cup.

42 Fronted by Boris Grebenshchikov, Aquarium was one of the most popular underground rock groups in the Soviet Union. Perestroika allowed them to breakthrough and achieve mass popularity in the mid-1980's.

43 *Gopnik* (plural *gopniki*) is the Russian word for a particular style of street thug who began to appear in the later years of the Soviet Union. *Gopniki* appear throughout Kozlov's fiction, including the novella and story collection entitled *Gopniki*.